THE BOX

ROBERT LIPMAN

This is a work of fiction. Any resemblance to actual events or persons, living or dead, is entirely coincidental.

Interior layout and design by Kuhn Design Group | www.KuhnDesignGroup.com
Cover and illustrations by Tom McGrath | www.SpikedMcGrath.com

Ordering Information:

Special discounts are available on quantity purchases by schools and other educational institutions. For details, contact the author at the email address above.

To my middle school students

CHAPTER 1

Max stared blankly at his seventh-grade class sched-ule. "Not Mr. North again! We just had him last year!"

"What's your problem?" Emile complained. "He gave you an A both semesters. I'm lucky to have gotten a C."

Max slipped a piece of gum into his mouth. "Yeah, but *you* always have to work for your grades. I don't!"

Max earned Egghead Club every year and got a special group picture in the school yearbook for the privilege. Anyone with a 4.0 average qualified, and Max always qualified, effortlessly. Emile was just the opposite. He ran his pens dry with ink spilled on notes from lectures he rarely fully understood. But he was used to it. Max never had to work—that is, except in Mr. North's class.

"Hey, look, it's Taco!" Max's eyes did a distanced high-five as Taco walked into class and planted himself in a seat near the back. A popular girl, Adrienne, entered after him, but she stood near the door waiting for her friends to come, and together they formed a private country club of desks—membership exclusive. Three new kids followed, and then came Swagger, a.k.a. Mr. Cool, who moseyed on up to the third row, high-fiving along the way. He fell comfortably into his last year's seat.

"North again, eh, Max?"

"Yeah. I'm bummed."

Mr. North was different from most teachers. For one thing, he was a genius who expected unending diligence from his students, assuming they were capable. If you didn't have it in you, he felt sorry for you and didn't push. But the harder you worked, the higher his expectations were. And, if he decided you were really smart, that was the end. Max had made a massively huge mistake by getting top marks on assignments during the first weeks of North's class last year, and for the rest of the year, he'd paid a heavy price for the honor. Besides the standard work, Max earned "enrichment activities" (work), and "supplemental test questions" (more work). For most everyone else, that kind of thing was just optional, for extra credit. But for students like Max, there was no getting around the supplementary work, because Mr. North was also grade counselor, which put him directly in charge of discipline and detention.

"Hey, look! It's Mustache!" Max stole a glance at the door, and there she was—Roxanne Buckfort, a familiar face at Woodwest Middle School. Teachers called her Roxie, but kids had dubbed her "Mustache" for the thin line of black hair above her lip that looked just like a mustache, even though she was a girl. Max felt bad for her, but he didn't want to call her Roxie in front of his friends, so he just didn't use any name for her at all if he could help it.

Mustache peered into the room, taking in which classmates she would have to contend with for the coming year. Then, sidling over to a spot closest to the door, she settled herself down, kicked her shoes off her feet, deep under her desk, and waited for Mr. North while fiddling with a zipper on her handbag.

Taco's quick imitation of Mustache had the boys in hysterics, especially when he tried tossing his shoes off and they just wouldn't go. Swagger, who was wearing slip-ons, gave a more successful demonstration, and with a swift thrust of both his knee and ankle sent his left shoe hurtling into the air and across the room just as Mr. North walked in.

Mr. North ignored the shoe, his eyeballs fixed steadily on each talker in the room until every desk was stone silent. Then he gave a brief greeting while circulating a six-page handout with a list of all of his rules. Students took turns reading those rules aloud. In keeping with his well-earned reputation, North then assigned a slew of homework before letting everyone go.

The rest of Max's first day passed without incident. It turned out that he, Emile, and Swagger shared all of the same classes, except math. Emile was lucky enough to be in low math—Mr. Durnham was really nice. They only saw

Taco for English and then for history with Mrs. Pinkston, a reptilian-looking teacher who never blinked or smiled. Everyone in seventh grade had Mr. Triggs for science and Mr. Schmitt for PE. But teachers, whoever they turned out to be in a given semester, were, as Max saw it, purveyors of useless worksheets and tests intended for no purpose other than to prove knowledge of information he knew deep down would have little use to him in real life.

CHAPTER 2

Max and Emile almost always walked home together. It was not an easy route. The walk itself would not have been so difficult except for the fact that there was an electric power generating station that blocked the way home from school, forcing an entirely unnecessary 30-minute hike up Hill Street just to get across to the other side. The only shortcut was by way of the old railroad tracks that ran between the main power station and a row of high-voltage transformers. Decades ago, when the local trains were shut down in favor of street bussing, the tracks had faded into obscurity and in time had turned seedy, squalid, and desolate. Nobody ever went in there.

Emile paused for a breather on the way home, pulling out a water bottle from his backpack. "Can you believe he gave homework on the first day?"

"I'd have trouble believing it if he *didn't* give homework

on the first day!" Max said. "But you can copy mine if you want. I finished it during science."

Emile sighed. "That's OK. If I'm ever going to learn anything, it's better that I just do it myself."

The boys eventually parted, and Max made his way home, stopping in the lobby of his building to grab the mail. With a last burst of energy for the day, Max jumped two flights of stairs and let himself into the empty two-bedroom apartment. The TV was still blasting from the morning. Max switched the channel, washed a plate from the sink, and served himself some canned fruit with cottage cheese. This was Max's regular daily routine, except for the canned fruit and cottage cheese, which was sometimes substituted with either frozen waffles, a frozen pizza, or a soup cup, unless his mom was home early with some leftovers from the restaurant where she worked as a waitress. But Mom had told Max she needed another late shift today, and Mr. North had not yet assigned Max any "special" homework assignments, so Max made do with the cottage cheese, watched television, and, for lack of any better options, went to sleep. *Maybe I'll have some interesting dreams...*

CHAPTER 3

Routine set in over the next month as classroom get-to-know-you parties evolved into actual academic work. Mr. North assigned his first major unit of vocabulary—seventy-five words—which Max memorized effortlessly in about a day, though he was careful not to let Mr. North know that. Mrs. Pinkston's class had been a breeze; for several days they played an ancient-culture bingo game she had picked up off the internet. Emile took it seriously, of course, while Max hid behind his own bingo board to polish off some homework from science. Everyone enjoyed PE except for Mustache, whose legs just didn't match the shorts students were forced to wear. All the teasing brought her to tears, and Mr. Schmitt had to send Swagger and another boy to Mr. North for a talk on bullying.

As Max and Emile were leaving school, Max could tell that Emile was deep in thought. That would happen periodically, and Max would just walk alongside quietly until

Emile was ready to open up. Finally, Emile broke his silence, clearing his throat as though preparing to share words of deep, profound wisdom, and then solemnly declared: "Max, this walk home is…ominous."

"Sorry, Emy," Max said. "It's not *ominous*, it's *arduous*. *Ominous* means 'threatening;' *arduous* is hardship and difficulty—like having to walk uphill, 30 minutes out of your way, to get somewhere we could be in less than five minutes if only we would walk along the tracks." Max pointed through the gate to the tracks. "You can even see my apartment from here if you look hard enough."

Emile squinted but couldn't see that far, even with glasses. "It's too dangerous, Max. There are bad stories about it, of people even getting killed. It's…it's…ominous!"

"No, it's not, and I'm not scared," Max grunted. "I'm sick and tired of climbing a mountain every day to get home."

The boys argued about this, but Emile was adamant, and though Max said he wasn't afraid, deep down he knew not to risk going on his own, at least not until he had fully explored it with someone else.

The first opportunity to enter was not long in coming. It happened one day a few weeks later when they reached the top of Hill Street only to discover that the road had been completely blocked off for repaving. Construction workers and traffic officers forbade passage to anyone, even tired and whiny schoolkids who had just walked the hill trying to get home. Emile took the setback in stride, but Max fumed as they retreated down to the bottom of the hill and landed themselves just outside the gates to the old tracks. Max chucked his backpack onto a bench, his eyes meanwhile trying to make out the shape of his building at the other end of the tracks.

"Now will you go with me, Emy?"

Emile shrugged weakly and continued putting up a fight, but Max could see that his friend's defenses were down, and after another few salvos, Emile finally acquiesced.

"Alright," he said softly, "but just this once."

Then, as inconspicuously as possible, the two boys slipped through the gate and faded into the distance.

CHAPTER 4

They walked quickly along the rails, Emile trembling, while Max took in as much of the scene as he could. It was hard to see anything, though. A row of utility buildings blocked the afternoon sun, making it unnaturally dark, and what light did shine down from above cast deep shadows off the power lines criss-crossing overhead. The electricity in the lines made a racket, and Emile, who was completely petrified, ran ahead of Max, urgently, with his hands cupped against his ears to keep out the loud buzzing of the wires. Soon they reached a clearing where the fence opened back onto the street, but before leaving, the boys parked themselves on a large, concrete drainage pipe lying there in the clearing, Emile peeking briefly into the hollow opening of the pipe to make sure nothing alive was lurking inside.

"Empty," Emile said with a relieved smile.

"See? There's nothing to be afraid of here," Max said. "Everything's perfectly fine."

Then, after a few more minutes of hanging around the clearing, they passed through the fence to the street and made their way home.

Before parting ways, the two boys stopped in front of Max's building. "Let's go back again tomorrow. OK, Emy?"

"Yeah, maybe. Have to think about it, though."

Over the next few days, Max (and even Emile) came to enjoy walking by way of the tracks. As they became more familiar with them, they slowed their pace and began to explore their surroundings. There was debris everywhere—old car tires, rusty metal rods, bricks. Max found an old barbell and tried to lift it over his head.

"Fifty pounds—I guess that's too heavy for me." He chucked it, barely missing Emile's foot.

Then, after winning a painful argument with a thorn-bush, Max seized an old bicycle that had apparently been discarded in a heap of junk. Its tires were flat, but they could roll well enough for Max to walk with it. Just then, Emile gasped, tugging urgently on Max's shirt.

"Something just moved in the plants back there, Max. I think we're being watched."

He pointed to some thick bushes against the wall of a building. Max peered into the bush as best he could without making it apparent that anything was amiss, and through a crevice in one of the many stalks of tall weeds, sure enough, he spotted the likeness of an eye staring back at them.

"Just keep walking, Emy. It's probably just an animal."

At first, they moved along the rails slowly, but caution quickly melted into outright panic, and they shot out of there as fast as they could to the fence at the clearing—the two boys and an old bike—and they made their way through to Reeves Street and then home.

CHAPTER 5

Max lugged the bike upstairs to his apartment and bent the wheels back into shape using his neighbor's tire kit. But by the time they turned smoothly enough to ride, the weather had also turned; it was pouring rain outside. So Max left the bike balanced against some cartons in his room, slid the dirty rags under his desk, and joined his mom for some leftovers that she had brought home from work.

"Here, I'll serve it, Mom. You've been making plates for people all day." Max scooped mashed potatoes from a plastic container and topped each serving with a piece of fried chicken schnitzel and a squirt of ketchup.

"Sure nice to be off my feet, Max. Anything new at school today?"

"Not really," Max lied, figuring that the tracks were, technically, *after* school, not *at* school. "Got an A+ on that vocabulary test North gave us."

"That's *Mr.* North, Max. He may not be your favorite, but

he *is* your teacher. Anyways, I'm glad to hear you're working hard," she added.

The storm was still going strong Monday morning, making the walk to school miserable, even though it was downhill. Max had every intention of cutting through the tracks that afternoon and had even gotten Emile's sworn promise to go with him. As far as Max was concerned, the days of walking up Hill Street were over, especially in the rain.

Rainy-day schedule was in effect at school, and all outdoor activities, including recess and PE, were cancelled. Cabin fever set in, and the teachers were in a real mood. That didn't bother Max, though. When it came to school, the only hard part, especially in bad weather, was the walk up Hill Street. Now, with the tracks as a viable shortcut, he was finally free to avoid the long walk once and for all. Besides, the tracks had a certain mystique that Max found uncannily seductive, and he couldn't wait to go back and see them again, even in the rain.

Nonetheless, Max lacked the self-confidence to enter such a secluded zone by himself, so he depended on Emile's willingness to go with him. And though he and Emile were the closest of friends, Emile was likely to self-reflect just a little too much. If left alone, he might even have a change of heart if Max weren't there to egg him on. So, to be sure Emile hadn't done too much thinking on his own, Max figured he had better find him before next period and reaffirm their plans for later that day. To Max's surprise and consternation, Emile was nowhere to be found, and he didn't show up to history class, either.

"Hey, Taco, where's Emy?"

"Went home. His grandmother picked him up early for a classical music performance in Uptown."

"WHAT?! That's so cheap! And he didn't even tell me!"

By dismissal time, the rain had picked up, assuredly just to spite Max, who felt betrayed and abandoned by his friend, even though he knew perfectly well that Emile hadn't actually done anything wrong. He grabbed his winter coat and backpack, and, with his mind racing, headed out to the street, his body soaking up the pouring rain as he pondered what to do.

Why can't I just go in there myself? I don't need him! He's just a coward anyway. The truth was, Max was deeply afraid to take the tracks without his friend, and he knew he was more of a coward even than Emy, which just made him angrier. Emy was small and kind of weak, but he was another person at least, and that made all the difference.

At the fence, Max tried to see past the tracks through the fog, but it was pretty dense.

What if there really had been someone hiding in the bushes last week?

Max started up Hill Street. As he trekked upward, the wind pressed hard against his body, pushing him backward as though laughing at him for even trying. The torrents of rain turned to hail, sharp bits of ice pinching at his cheeks.

Several minutes of climbing against the wind yielded Max little progress, and his face reddened with each step. The last straw for Max came in the form of a pickup truck that saw fit to steer over an accumulating river of rainwater flowing downhill below the sidewalk curb, and, as luck would have it, executed a brilliant mini-tsunami at the exact location where Max was busy struggling to hike. Waves of water plummeted down on him, knocking him to the ground and sending his backpack into a patch of wet, muddy gravel. Irate, Max picked himself up and stormed down the hill to the fence. His mind was made up.

CHAPTER 6

Once Max had slipped through the fence and advanced toward the protective buildings to the side of the tracks, the rain showers eased, and a drop in wind chill warmed the air. Heavy cloud cover choked off most of the sunlight, though, and Max, upset with himself for not bringing a flashlight, struggled against the fog as he made his way toward the clearing on the other side.

Making a mental note to search for more treasure once the clouds cleared, Max pressed forward through the mist, his mind intensely focused on where he was going. He couldn't hear beyond the electric wires overhead, which buzzed furiously, the wires deeply disturbed by rainwater seeping into the transformer boxes and shorting the circuits. If not for all the noise, Max might have been more alert to the angry rustling of bushes and the displeased pair of eyes peering at him from behind. Suddenly, with no warning, a deep, piercing voice rang out.

"Thieeeeef! Thieeeeef! Kill the thief who stole my bicycle!"

Max turned, gazing for a terrifying instant at the massive form rising from the bushes, and, in sheer panic, bolted headfirst into the fog. The figure gave chase, and Max leaped forward, slamming into a tree before catching himself and regaining his stride. Max remembered that there was a bend in the road ahead, and though he didn't know exactly where, he apparently guessed correctly, given the fact that he did not ram into a wall. Afraid to slow down even to catch his breath, Max dove forward at a frenzied pace toward light from what he thought might be the place where the clearing met the fence.

Finally he reached the clearing, twisting desperately to avoid colliding with the old concrete pipe, but just as he was in range of the fence, he stumbled over a discarded metal barbecue grill and fell, arms flailing, face forward into the dirt, pain searing up his ankle.

Realizing he would never reach the fence in time, and unable to stand up because of the pain, Max crawled for cover, and within moments he had crept into the narrow opening of the concrete pipe in the clearing before blacking out.

CHAPTER 7

When Max awakened, it took time for him to realize where he was. Ears perked, he listened for voices outside the concrete pipe, but all he could hear was the electric buzzing of the overhead wires. Avoiding any motion that could attract attention, he tried directing his eyes toward the entrance to the pipe to see if anyone was looking in, but he couldn't see anything because it was pitch black outside.

He felt a deep sense of unease at the idea of staying where he was, and as his thinking cleared, he came to the rather unpleasant realization that he was not the only thing alive in that pipe, and that something large was lying next to him...and breathing.

Max flinched, but when he tried to push himself away and toward the opening, a cold hand grasped his wrist and pulled down sharply. Instinctively, Max shot his free arm forward in defense, but it too was seized and held tight by another set of icy fingers. The thing then coiled its legs around

Max's body, cobra-like, and held firm against any resistance Max could muster. Max's protests soon melted into cries of despair and whimpering, which continued for some number of minutes until finally, in a quiet, raspy voice, It spoke.

"You dare not go."

It held tightly against Max's body and did not release its hold.

"Why not?"

"I told them you got away. You dare not go yet," It repeated, releasing Max's hands. "If you wait quietly, I will tell you when to go."

Max did just as It said.

"Who are you?" Max whispered.

It sighed. "I am Nothing."

"Um. Well, I'm Max." Max tried his best to stay on Its good side. "I was on my way home from school and got chased for stealing someone's bicycle, which I found in a heap."

Max turned back to his own thoughts. He wasn't as scared now. After all, his new acquaintance had helped him to escape. But his body still ached, and he worried about getting home before his mom did. Besides, it was pitch black, and he was kind of stuck with a complete stranger who might just be a zombie.

"Why did you come here?" the thing asked, cutting the silence short.

It listened intently as Max shared his frustrations and reasons for cutting through the tracks. It seemed to appreciate

Max's interest in the tracks, and especially how much risk Max took to avoid the difficulties of the normal walk home.

"There is something I would like to show you," It said.

Max looked up. Of course, he couldn't see anything in the dark. But gradually, the inner walls of the concrete pipe began to glow. A subtle green hue appeared, which was attractive and wondrous, though the light itself did not actually brighten the inside of the concrete pipe in a way that would make seeing other things easier. The glow intensified, though, imparting a mesmerizing display of light against the pipe's cylindrical walls, and Max became deeply transfixed by its beauty. As the light increased, it revealed amazing intricacy in design. There were hundreds, if not thousands, of web-like lines, like threads of silk made of laser beams, each connected one to another, forming a brilliant luminescent matrix. The longer he gazed at the pattern, the more he seemed to see deeper connections and more complex designs. Max was entranced and would have remained so had the spectacle not faded back into the darkness after only a few minutes.

Needless to say, Max was extremely impressed.

"That was amazing! How did you do that?" he asked.

"It was an Orb," the thing replied. "I get them every day, and they are both beautiful and extraordinarily potent."

"But where does it come from?" Max had already decided he wanted to have his own Orbs.

"There is just one source in the entire world for such beautiful Orbs, and it is in my pocket. If you like, you may have it."

"What?! You're giving me your Orbs?"

"No. It is impossible to capture an Orb, much less give one, but I will give you the Box that *makes* the Orbs, on condition that the ownership of the Box changes permanently from me to you once you accept it."

Max was dubious. After all, he was no sucker, and he wasn't about to be tricked into buying a fancy flashlight, especially from a complete stranger who was living in a pitch-black cement cylinder. On the other hand, it would really be cool to make more of those Orbs.

"What do you get out of it?" he asked slyly. "I'm not paying any money."

"There is no cash payment. It no longer works for me as it once did, and I am happy to be rid of it if you will take it."

The thing reached into its pocket, retrieved the Box, and placed it squarely in Max's hand.

Max thanked him. "It certainly will give me something interesting to play around with."

"Well, it is yours now," the thing said. "And it is safe for you to go home."

"What about you?" Max asked. "Do you live here?"

"Not now," It said. "I'm just passing through."

Max could see no harm in taking a free box, especially one that made Orbs. So he said his thank-yous, stashed the object in his pocket, slid cautiously out of the pipe, and hobbled home.

CHAPTER 8

The stairs were brutal on Max's ankle, but with some hopping and pulling on the handrail, Max finally managed to reach his apartment. Before long, he had showered and was chilling in bed with some music blaring to blunt the pain. The Box sat in his pants pocket, out of mind for the time being, since the first matter of concern was coming up with some excuse to explain the scratches on his face once his mom got home. He settled on blaming a fall in the bushes at school for both the scratches and the ankle, and his explanation turned out to be more than satisfactory.

"Oh my, let me see your face, Maxy." His mom applied some ointment to the wounds and served Max some hot cocoa. "And you had to wait for me all this time to get home."

"I'm fine, Mom, really!"

"Just the same. If I didn't have to be at work so much, I could take care of you, you know." She sighed. "It didn't have to be this way."

Max pretended not to hear her. He knew his mother's difficulties and didn't feel up to dealing with them. He had his own problems.

For several nights, post-trauma anxiety curbed any possibility of Max getting solid sleep, even though he was desperate for slumber. Nodding off meant rehashing the terrible chase, the fall, the darkness, the creature in the pipe, and the Orb. Then came the deafening buzz of imaginary electric wires overhead, which woke him up in a panic. Max barely functioned in school from lack of sleep. Fortunately, there was a sub in for Mr. North, who was out with flu; math class was just a review of square roots from last year that half the class had forgotten, and videos occupied most of science class. Emile could tell something was off with Max, but Max didn't want to talk about it; and strangely, from Emile's point of view, Max made no further effort to cut through the tracks after school.

Max didn't get around to examining the Box until the weekend, but having felt it in his pocket, he was already aware of its square shape and the large hole through the middle of it, which was wide enough to fit almost two of his fingers. When he looked at it in the light, though, he found the Box to be made of wood, perfectly smooth with a gleaming varnish. There were no switches or knobs to be found, and as much as Max searched, he could not locate a compartment to hold batteries, or, for that matter, find anything that resembled a plug or socket to power a laser projector. Tapping it or even pounding it against his desk didn't activate anything, and there were no apparent secret compartments in case it was intended to be a magic trick.

How is this supposed to work without some kind of lens or laser projector? he thought as he chucked the thing onto his desk for the night. *Well, at least I didn't pay money for it.*

CHAPTER 9

A month went by, and though Max found sleep less elusive than before, his dreams remained vivid. One such dream especially captured his attention, though. It began with the chase through the tracks, as usual, and then the fall and the cement pipe. But at the point when Max saw the light, the vision evolved from light appearing against the interior of the pipe, to the light of a glowing sphere suspended like a helium balloon over his bed. Furthermore, after he had watched this for a few minutes, it became readily apparent that this Orb he was seeing was real, and was, in fact, floating in his room. Upon this realization, Max bolted into a sitting position and looked up with a start. There in the darkness was indeed an Orb of epic beauty, its light forming a three-dimensional spiral whorl of soft-colored yet intense green laser, which combined into the visible shape of a perfect, brilliantly illuminated sphere. He lay still, admiring it, and then watched it evaporate into the darkness.

Realizing immediately that the Box had to have played a part in this, Max sprung from his bed and snapped on the lights. Grabbing hold of the Box, he scoured it for clues of openings or secrets to its inner workings, to no avail. He thought maybe it would help to shake the thing, and vigorously thrust it to and fro. Nothing. Then he tried tapping it from all directions and pressing his ear against it to see if it was hollow, but it seemed totally solid except for the hole in the middle. Oddly, though, there seemed to be a faint whisper coming from that hole whenever Max's ear approached it, sort of like the sound of the turning of air from a seashell. The mysterious murmuring caused Max to give the Box a hard shake and listen. This time what he heard was distinct and significantly louder.

"Kindly..."

Huh? Max thought, as he heard what sounded like a distinguishable word. He shook it once more and again listened closely.

"Stop..."

"Hey," Max surmised, "this is like a draw-string doll that talks when you pull on it." He shook the Box again and listened.

"Shaking. Me!" The word "me" seemed hurriedly fit in.

"Kindly...Stop...Shaking...Me," Max repeated to himself.

"Kindly stop shaking me. Oh," he said. "It doesn't want to be shaken!"

Max pressed his lips against the hole, calling out in a loud voice, "O—K. Ve—ry. Sor—ry." He listened for a response.

The voice spoke again, this time with greater coherence. Having not been shaken, it was apparently in better condition to speak, and that is just what it proceeded to do.

"Firstly," it expressed sternly, "let's establish some rules. You might want to get something to write with."

Max got a pen and noted the following rules as prescribed that evening by the voice in the Box:

1. Do not shake me, ever! It makes me nauseous.

2. Kindly refrain from yelling into my hole. I can hear you just fine at normal speaking levels. I'm no idiot, and I'm not deaf.

3. I am not to be awakened at night when I am sleeping.

4. Tell no one of my powers, or you will get no further benefit from them.

Oh, and…

5. Do not chew mint-flavored gum in here—I can't stand the smell.

"Now, if you don't mind," the Box added, "it is the middle of the night. I'm going back to sleep."

And with that, Max had no choice but to put the Box back on his desk and go back to bed, where he lay still…thinking.

CHAPTER 10

Max slept right through his alarm clock and woke up with a start. Because it was so late, there was no time to try communicating with the Box again, as much as Max would have liked to. He thought of possibly playing sick that day, but there was a test in math, and Mr. North was expecting to meet with him that day, probably to assign him extra work or something.

In keeping with the rules set forth by the Box, Max said nothing about his encounters with it to anyone, including Swagger and Emile. He had plenty to talk to them about, though.

It turned out that Mr. North was so impressed with Max's essay on *The Giver* that he had asked Max to write his own dystopian story as a required "enrichment activity." Max was furious. He fumed for the rest of the day, incensed by the sheer injustice of the extra work, and only got back to thinking about the Box once he got home and noticed it sitting on his desk.

"How about a dystopian novel about an evil English teacher who takes over the world and assigns useless homework to everyone in the society for no reason," he considered rather seriously.

With that, he picked up the Box as though it were a fortune-telling eight ball, and, pressing his lips to it and speaking softly, he asked, "Hey, Box, what do you think I should write about?"

The Box vibrated quietly.

Max went on to vent to the Box about the circumstances of his relationship with Mr. North, and how Mr. North kept assigning him new "enrichment" projects that he hated getting. Max held the Box tightly in his fist as he spoke, and suddenly the Box chimed in.

"And if you don't perform well on his assignments?" it asked.

"That has never happened," he admitted. "Mr. North only gives enrichment to kids who impress him with good work."

"In that case, the answer is obvious," the Box reasoned. "Don't impress him with good work. Remember, boy, subpar work still passes the course."

That's novel, Max thought, taken aback, as he pondered how to actually perform subpar work. As a skill, this was something he had never done.

Over the next several weeks, Max made a vigorous effort

to perform poorly on work assigned by Mr. North. To assist in the ruse, the Box gave Max advice on how to gradually decrease his work performance without making it seem sudden or deliberate. Still, it was very difficult for Max to keep up the pretense.

Max took to speaking more with the Box about school, friends, and whatever else was on his mind. The Box took great interest in what Max had to say, especially when Max shared personal challenges and frustrations. It bothered Max, though, that while the Box was learning so much about him, he knew very little about it. He worried that the Box might be dangerous, or an instrument of some evil warlord, and the Box's answers to his questions only intensified his concerns.

"Are you a Horcrux, like from Harry Potter?" Max asked one afternoon, trying not to sound like an inquisitor.

The Box chuckled. "I am no Horcrux," it said. "A Horcrux is but a mere fraction of a soul. I embody the dreams and aspirations of *many* souls."

Max, who did not fully grasp the ramifications of the Box's answer, continued his interrogation.

"Well, how do I know if you're good or evil?"

The Box scoffed, evidently not taking well to that line of questioning or Max's tone of voice.

"How do I know if *you* are good or evil?" the Box retorted. "Other than what you've told me, the only thing I know about *you* is that you steal bicycles!"

"I do not!" Max shouted. He glanced briefly at the bike leaning against the wall of his bedroom.

With that, the Box abruptly broke off the conversation and refused to discuss the matter further. There was a still silence for several minutes before the Box spoke up again, this time in a sweet and very agreeable tone of voice.

"I am spinning something very special just for you," it said as it began to vibrate quietly. "It is an Orb, and it will be ready tonight, but not until 2 a.m. Once it floats, touch your nose to it, and you shall experience its immense powers."

The Box's sudden change in attitude caught Max by surprise, but he was nonetheless delighted at the prospect of seeing another Orb like the one he had woken up to the previous evening.

"How will I reach it?" Max asked.

"*No problemo*, my boy! This Orb is a special gift for you, and it will seek you just as you desire it. Now, if you don't mind, I must be left alone. Spinning Orbs is not easy."

CHAPTER 11

Max had no trouble keeping occupied while he waited for his Orb. His mom had gotten home early from the restaurant and was both alert enough that evening to notice that Max had not yet scrubbed down the grates of the stove in the kitchen, and awake enough to enforce that the task be addressed promptly. On any other day, Max would have minded the grueling work, but to his mother's delight, he totally embraced it this particular evening because it kept him busy all of that time.

"You're maturing so nicely, Maxy darling."

To distract himself from the long wait, Max went well beyond the grates, wiping down the refrigerator shelves, emptying the cabinets under the sink, and spraying for bugs. Predictably, his mom disappeared to bed by about midnight, but Max kept working and didn't stop for another hour and a half. With thirty minutes remaining, Max dashed to his room, showered long enough to kill another fifteen minutes, jumped into pajamas, and then waited on his bed for the last ten minutes with his eyes glued firmly on the Box.

Sure enough, at precisely 2 a.m., a trickle of mist began rising into the air from the hole in the Box, and Max was quickly captivated by its gentle beauty. He watched as the mist arranged itself into a perfect lighted sphere. Unlike the Orb he had seen hovering near the ceiling over his bed, this Orb floated at face level, swaying in place as if to prompt Max to touch it. The allure was considerable, and though Max did have some nagging concerns over his choice to engage with the Box's Orb, these concerns were brushed aside as he reached, guardedly, with the tip of his nose to the surface of the Orb in front of him and touched it. At once, the Orb's lights shimmered and the sphere moved, positioning itself around Max's head like a translucent virtual reality helmet.

What followed was beyond the imagination. Strands of undulating laser circulated vigorously in an almost dizzying spiral before Max's eyes, creating a hyper-drive space zoom effect that drew Max's attention deeper and deeper into a dazzling whorl of intense color against a background of mist. Echoing sounds of distant purring cleansed and washed away any feelings of anxiety and concern, leaving Max's mind and body free to experience fully immersive euphoric sensations.

The mist, which had been obscuring Max's view of the interior of the Orb with its glorious array of reflected colors, then ascended to the top of the Orb, where it condensed and heated up like steam, hovering in a small, effervescent cloud. Without mist in the main chamber, Max could now see from his vantage point at the center of the Orb to the inner surface of the sphere, where, posted in large, neon lettering, were the words "DREAM HACKER," and in small print just below, the subtitle "VERSION 13.2.12.102." A virtual dashboard offered TARGET and SETTING indicators, along with lighted panels marked HACK AS SELF and HACK AS CHARACTER. There was also a time meter that read "15 MINUTES." A robotic-sounding voice echoed through the chamber: "Dream Hacker is now ready; name your target."

Though Max was quick to gather the entertaining implications of what was before him, he wasn't sure exactly what to do to begin.

"Um. Um. Hmm," Max said.

The voice cut in again. "Dream Hacker Help On: You have fifteen minutes of Local Play. Long-distance hacking times depend on location and circumstances of the target dreamer. Time is also affected by modifying the setting of a dream or by inserting characters, including yourself. Refer to the steam-meter at any time for your current remaining play. Dream Hacker works best when the target is in REM sleep, which occurs most often during the first 90 minutes of sleep, and non-REM stage 3, which lasts for several hours thereafter. Results may vary. Say 'repeat' to hear this message again."

After a short pause, the voice returned: "Dream Hacker is now ready; name your target."

Max grinned deviously. "Um, Swagger," he said.

CHAPTER 12

A thin current of steam drifted from the cloud over Max's head to the dashboard, which affected a slight drop in the meter level to initialize the process. At once, to Max's surprise and delight, the chamber came alive with throngs of spectators watching, screaming, and chanting from the bleachers while players huddled on the field.

Apparently, in Swagger's dream, the pitcher had loaded the bases and, on account of an injury on the last throw, was now being removed. The scene carried on.

A combined aroma of Cracker Jacks, hot dogs, and beverages wafted about in drifts within the Orb, and stadium billboards plastered over the bleachers along the walls of the sphere blasted congratulatory messages to fans as the organ played uber-excited charge-to-victory songs. The huddle continued while giant OLED displays splashed beer ads, and a helicopter overhead broadcasted live coverage of the event. The home team was leading six to five in the

AUTOMOTIVE
MCGEVER
01
S

ninth inning, bases loaded, with two outs and a full count. The next pitch would decide everything: the game, the series, and ultimately, which team would be recipient of the World Series Trophy. The fans, in an ebullient frenzy, bellowed vociferously for the new pitcher. After all, they knew well who was on deck to throw the winning pitch. Chants ensued. "Swagger, Swagger, Swagger, Swagger…" they called as the precocious thirteen-year-old ascended from the dugout and marched toward the mound. A quick nod quieted the crowds as he wound up for the winning pitch, unleashing the best two-seam fastball in the history of the game. Crowds of fans stormed the field as the winning team lifted Swagger McGevery into the air to celebrate the triumphant save. Even the losing players on the other team couldn't help but congratulate the young athlete for his brilliant pitch.

Then the setting changed in a swirl of mist, and Max noted that there were just five more minutes of play on the meter.

The scene turned to the schoolyard. Adrienne was standing at the drinking fountain alone as Swagger approached from the courtyard. Max moved closer to listen.

"Adrienne, I was just thinking that maybe we could go get ice cream after school?" Swagger asked.

That's gutsy, Max thought, *though if anyone would get a yes from her, it would be Swagger.* He looked up at the meter to check his play time—four minutes—and while doing so, caught sight of the nearby HACK AS CHARACTER indicator on the dashboard, which gave him a brilliantly wicked idea.

"Hack as Adrienne," Max tried.

The indicator blinked ADRIENNE in red, and at once, to Max's astonishment, every move he made, and every word he uttered, was instantly cloned in the dream by Max-Adrienne.

"Um, I don't think so," Max-Adrienne replied. "I was really hoping to do homework, with, um, Max."

"MAX!?" Swagger snorted. "Why would you do homework with HIM when you could go for ice cream with ME?!"

Feigning a deep cough to stifle an impending bout of hysterical laughter, Max-Adrienne explained, "Well, you know. Max is just SO-O-O smart."

Max was about to bring the point home again when the chamber abruptly turned gray, and a voice announced that the allotted time was over. Sure enough, when Max checked, the meter read zero, and the cloud of steam above Max's head had fully dissipated.

Then the sphere itself slowly evaporated, its color scheme growing gentle and mild, leaving Max encased in a warm blanket of serenity and comfort as he pondered who he might like to hack next time.

CHAPTER 13

In the morning, Max said nothing to Emile about the Orb or the dream hacking. Besides not wanting to disobey the Box's rule, he wondered if Emile would have appreciated the humor in it. After all, dreams are supposed to be a private matter, and Emile likely would not have approved. In any case, Max's main concern involved spying out Swagger and catching him for a word before class. True, the Box strictly prohibited his revealing the Orb's powers to anyone, but that didn't mean, necessarily, that he couldn't have some fun without revealing too much. Besides, Max really wanted to know if the Dream Hacker's targets were real, and if the dreams themselves were vivid enough to be remembered upon wakening. So, when Swagger rode his bike to the designated area in the yard, Max made sure to be there to find out.

"Oh, Swag. Have a minute?"

"Sure, Max. What's up?"

Pretending not to remember that Swagger had baseball practice that afternoon, Max whipped out a "two scoops for the price of one" card. "Just wondering if you wanna go after school to get some…ice cream?"

"Can't, Max. I've got baseball practice." Swagger pulled up his shirt to reveal his team jersey underneath, emphasizing the point.

"Oh, OK. I guess I'll just do…homework," Max shared. "Hmm, anyone you think might like to do homework with me?" he added, watching Swagger carefully for any sign of recognition or memory of the dream.

Swagger's reaction was swift, silent, and sullen, as he bit his lip and stared at the ground in blank confusion. Apparently, he remembered the dream quite well. Realizing now how vivid the dream had been, and the distress he had caused his friend, Max straightaway regretted having brought up the subject, and was only too thankful when, just then, the school bell rang and they both had to run to class.

The day went from bad to worse when Max realized he had completely forgotten about the first draft of his *Giver* assignment, and of course Mr. North called him out on that. Mr. North also assigned Max a monstrous list of advanced literary terms to learn, the knowledge of which (Mr. North insisted) would enhance Max's life for years to come, and, incidentally, was due in less than a week. Max, sporting a fake smile, took the worksheets, stuffed them into his backpack, and grumbled to Emile about them all the way home.

CHAPTER 14

Wondering whose dreams he might hack next, Max flew up the stairs to his apartment and darted straight to his room without even stopping at the fridge for food. Besides the exhilaration and excitement of the dream hacking, Max also hoped for more of that warm feeling of comfort he had experienced with the prior Orb to wash away his mounting frustrations with Mr. North. The only question was if the Box would be willing to spin him a new Orb. To that end, Max decided to engage the Box first in general conversation and then, when the time was right, ask for an Orb if the Box hadn't already offered him one by then. So Max told the Box all about his day at school, and particularly about the list of literary terms Mr. North was forcing him to learn. While Max poured his heart out, the Box just listened, purring quietly to itself, until Max finished speaking.

"The literary test is insignificant," the Box declared. "Passing it should be a breeze."

"But there are over two hundred terms to study!" Max retorted, his voice higher in pitch.

The Box's voice grew stern. "Would you like my help or not?"

Max agreed to receive the help and followed the Box's instructions exactly as he was told. First, as directed, he detached a blank sheet of paper from his notebook and set it down on the desk. Next, he placed the Box on top of the blank page as though the Box were acting as a paperweight. Then, as instructed, he dragged the Box firmly against the paper to the right, to the left, and then up and down. Noticing only a small change in hue on the blank page, Max continued vigorously "scrubbing" the paper with the bottom of the Box, back and forth, back and forth, repeatedly, until, finally, he saw what appeared to be a decipherable word on the page.

"Meter," the print read.

With further rubbing, Max made out more of the text. "Iambic meter."

"Iambic meter?" Max repeated to himself.

After over two and a half hours of vigorous pressing, rubbing, and scrubbing, all of the print on the page had finally sharpened enough to be legible. The title read *Literary Terms: An Assessment*, then, an inch or two below the title, a test prompt printed in bold text. It said,

Define the following ten literary terms and give an example of how each term is used in literature.

1. *Allusion:*

2. *Assonance:*

3. *Contrast:*

4. *Foreshadowing:*

5. *Iambic meter:*

6. *Trochaic meter:*

7. *Irony:*

8. *POV:*

9. *Tone:*

10. *Voice:*

Astonished and dumbfounded, Max stared silently at what was obviously an exact copy of the literary terms assessment Mr. North had prepared or was in the process of preparing for him.

"How did you do that?! Now all I have to do is learn what these ten words are, and I'll pass the test…This is amazing!"

The Box chuckled. "Actually, you will only need to study seven words. If you learn all ten, your teacher will think the test was too easy, and he'll give you another list to learn. Less than seven and he'll assume you didn't try. Seven is the magic number."

"Seven," Max repeated. "Um, and speaking of magic, would it be at all possible to, um, make me another of those magical Orbs?"

The Box did not answer. It vibrated quietly to itself for several minutes while Max waited. When it finally did reply, the response was not as Max had expected.

"I will trade you," the Box declared. "You provide me a share of your intellectual prowess, and I will give you more access to my Orbs."

"You want a share of my what?" Max asked.

The Box purred. "Your intellectual prowess," it repeated. "I am always interested in having a share of the talents of my clients, and since you are very smart, I would like some of your work in exchange for some of my mine. It's a fair trade."

"No, it isn't," Max said, smacking the Box against the desk. "I'm not giving you any of my smartness."

The Box vibrated silently and then conjured a puff of red mist from its middle that smelled of burnt cigar. "Have it your way," it said.

Max spent the rest of the day second-guessing how he could have played his conversation differently with the Box so that he could have ended up getting a new Orb. Now, at this impasse, it seemed there was nothing to be done. Max was, however, curious to see if the Box would spin another of its own floating type of Orbs—the kind that he had seen previously hovering near the ceiling. So, over the next few nights, Max either stayed up or set a pillow alarm to wake him in time to confirm that the Box was indeed producing Orbs reliably every night at 2 a.m.

I wonder what would happen if I touched one of those, Max thought with a shrewd smile. *They're in my room, so they kind of belong to me.*

CHAPTER 15

Floating Orbs presented a significant logistical challenge for Max in that they were high up near the ceiling and therefore hard to reach. Max didn't own a ladder, but he did have a desk large and sturdy enough to support a chair on top of it, which he tested the next day after school for height. Sure enough, standing tall on the chair, he had no trouble reaching his nose to the area just below the ceiling of his room. Of course, in all of this, he didn't say a word to the Box or to anyone else.

The next night, as soon as he felt his pillow alarm, he quickly positioned himself near the ceiling in the corner of the room where the Orb had migrated each of the prior few nights. He waited, but on this occasion, unfortunately, when the Orb floated to the ceiling, it drifted in the opposite direction, far from Max or his desk and chair, and was completely out of reach. Realizing that dragging the desk across the room at that hour of the night would make too much noise, Max had no choice but to dismantle his make-shift ladder and to try again another night.

Did the Orb deliberately steer away from me? Max wondered.

The revelation happened in science the next day while Mr. Triggs was droning on about cell mutations.

"It was the window!" Max gasped, completely forgetting that he was supposed to be listening to Triggs.

"Cells don't have windows," Mr. Triggs barked. He hated when students interrupted his train of thought. "Max, would you see me during recess, please?"

Mr. Triggs had been in an obnoxious mood all class, but Max had more important things to think about, and he didn't care about staying after anyway. It turned out, he realized, that he had closed his window in the afternoon to keep down the noise when he moved the desk and had not reopened it at night when he went to sleep. Air circulation from the open window would certainly have pushed the Orb nearer to him. Tonight, with the window open, Max figured, the Orb would be his.

CHAPTER 16

At 2 a.m. that night, clad in his pajamas, Max mounted the chair atop his desk and stood, primed, perched, and ready for the Orb to materialize. Sure enough, the Box spun the most beautiful Orb he had ever seen. Wasting no time, Max touched his nose to the alluring sphere, prompting the Orb to immediately form around his head and envelope him just as had happened previously with the Orb he had received from the Box as a gift.

Pulsating lights within the shelter of the encompassing sphere flickered before his eyes in perfect, symphonic harmony as incoherent whispers spoke quietly in his ears. Lights whirred across his visual periphery at dizzying speeds, and Max had to steady himself on the chair in order not to fall.

Max's eyes and thoughts were drawn deep into the colorful mist as it swirled around him, superceding his worries and frustrations with sensations of peace and comfort. Then the mist condensed, turning to steam and revealing

the Dream Hacker dashboard and the time meter as the now-familiar voice echoed, "Dream Hacker is now ready; name your target."

Max decided not to target friends, considering what had happened with Swagger. *Let's try a teacher.* "How about Mr. Triggs!" he suggested.

With a drop in the meter, the steam-powered hacking engine revved up, and Max found himself in a hardware store. A younger Mr. Triggs was at the counter, matching bolts with screws and distributing the various pieces into a compartmentalized display in one of the shopping aisles.

Wow, his dreams are as boring as his lectures are, Max thought as a stream of vapor swept the scene and replaced it with a more current Mr. Triggs, planting daffodils in his garden. The meter level dropped again as the scene changed first to Mr. Triggs taking a bubble bath and then to Mr. Triggs grading papers. *He must live really far away if the meter is almost out already.* The meter emptied the last of its steam with an image of his teacher getting a tooth extracted at the dentist. *Oh well,* Max thought. *At least now I know that these floating Orbs can also hack dreams.*

As the Orb dissipated, it left Max feeling relaxed and positive, which he came to look forward to. Granted, not every Orb let Max hack dreams, but they always felt really good. In fact, during much of the day, Max enjoyed the continual sense of serenity bestowed on him the night before by the previous Orb. This lasted until about sundown and then waned steadily as Max began feeling anxious and stressed. This hit Max hardest at about the time his mom arrived home. The dismal feeling stayed with him until the next night's Orb, and in the meantime, it wasn't hard for his mother to notice that Max felt unwell.

"Are you OK, Maxy? You seem so nervous."

"I'm OK, Mom," Max lied. "Just tired." He watched as she shoveled peels from the counter into the trashcan.

"I try so hard to do good for you, Maxy." Her voice trailed off. "But without your father…"

Max straightened up. "I'm *fine*, Mom. Really! Nothing to do with him. He left and that's it. You have to move on."

"That's what I've always told ya, Max, but it's not quite like that. It's for when you're older. Then you'll understand."

"It's not quite like *what*, Mom? Why isn't he here then?"

"It's not time to tell you. When you're older, Max, I will. I promise."

Max had never questioned the story of his father's departure before. Now, he felt lied to.

It was on Friday morning that Max submitted Mr. North's literary terms test, answering seven of the words correctly, just as the Box had advised him to do. One answer he left blank, and the others he mixed up definitions from other words on the list so that he would get them wrong. Yet Mr. North seemed happy enough not to make Max redo the test, just as the Box had predicted. Max also turned in his dystopian narrative, but, having not received sage council from the Box, Max wasn't sure if his submission would fully convince his teacher that the lackluster quality of it was the best that he could do. Seeing that he and the Box were not presently on the best terms, all he could do was turn in the work without trying too hard and just hope it would be good enough to pass. So that's what he did. Mr. North flipped through the story quickly but said he would have to give it a careful read later.

Emile was out with a cold that day, so after class, Max

and Swagger hit the cafeteria line, just the two of them. During class, Swagger had been uncharacteristically quiet and more pensive than Max had ever seen him. In fact, Swagger was so out of it that he even got good conduct marks from Mr. North, and not one demerit all morning. In fact, the teachers were all too thrilled by Swagger's quiet and well-behaved disposition. Max worried, though, that Swagger had not been acting like himself since the incident of the hacked dream and that Swagger might even harbor bad feelings on account of Adrienne. But while Max sat fumbling with a cheese sandwich and trying to figure out what to say, Swagger interjected.

"Uh, Max," Swagger said softly, his eyes glued to his bowl of spaghetti bolognaise. "I was thinking. Next time you're looking for someone to do homework with…" He gulped. "You might try asking…Adrienne."

"Adrienne?" Max repeated.

"Yeah, Max, Adrienne," he said. "She might be interested."

Max looked away. He hardly felt deserving right now of a friend like Swagger. Apparently, Swagger had taken the dream very—maybe too—seriously. "Thanks, Swag, but I think she's made for you."

"I don't think so, Max."

The argument was cut short by Taco, who was sitting a few tables over. He called out to Max. "Who is? Who's made for who?" Then other kids joined the chorus until the bell rang a few minutes later.

Disappointed in himself over what he had done to Swagger, Max returned to class only to find that he had been summoned to Mr. North's office. This was not good; Max knew that Mr. North had probably already read through his dystopian narrative.

"I'm so disappointed in this work, Max. It's sloppy."

"Disappointed" was one of Mr. North's favorite words when it came to kids whose work didn't make the cut, and knowing this, Max had a habit of always counting the number of times in a given class session that Mr. North used it to describe underperformers. This time was different, though, because the rebuke was aimed at Max, but as Max saw it, the assignment itself was unfair and forced upon him for no reason. So, thirteen "disappointeds," a "displeased," and a "dissatisfied" later, Max left Mr. North's office, fuming.

I'll be seeing you in your dreams, Mr. North. Max smiled grimly as he plotted his revenge.

CHAPTER 18

Aside from the scavenging of rats and other various wildlife in the alley below, all was quiet that evening on Reeves Street. Night life had never really taken shape in this quiet neighborhood where Max and his mother lived, and in the small hours of the night, the entire apartment complex was practically a graveyard buried deeply in quiet slumber. Alone in his room, yet very much awake, Max stood balanced upon the chair atop his desk, bathing in the familiar cascade of euphoric sensations as his nose touched the perimeter of the Orb, his view occluded by the heavy drape of mist. The brilliant luminescent display that followed was brief—a good sign, Max thought, that a dream hacking dashboard was in fact concealed behind the wall of mist. Of particular interest to Max this evening was the SETTING indicator—a tool that, according to the Orb's help message, would force the dreamer to dream the content of

Max's choice. Max had spent most of the day designing the perfect dream setting—one that would afford him the richest opportunity to put Mr. North in his place and right the wrong that had been perpetrated earlier that day. Finally, when the mist lifted, the dashboard appeared, and a familiar voice could be heard speaking.

"Dream Hacker is now ready. Name your target."

"Setting," Max guessed.

"Dream Hacker Help On," the voice responded. "To access the dream fabrication module, use syntax as follows: 'Target [Name of Target] Setting.' Then follow the prompts. Dream Hacker is now ready. Name your target."

"Um…Target, Mr. North, Setting," Max tried.

A small stream of mist flowed from the cloud over Max's head to the SETTING indicator, affecting an immediate yet subtle reduction in active hacking time just to initialize the sequence.

"Do you grant permission for Dream Hacker to access and retrieve a mind-print of your desired setting? Say 'Allow' to grant permission or 'Cancel' to exit."

"Allow," Max consented.

The voice continued, "When prompted, be sure to have the desired setting visualized in mind as clearly as possible. On count of…five, four, three, two, one." *Click.*

A flurry of mist encircled the periphery of the Orb, swirling to and fro, each gust bringing intricate new detail to the interior appearance of Dolby Hall, Los Angeles, California, home of the Academy Awards. The place looked just as Max had seen it on TV and imagined it during the mind-print the Orb had taken as Dream Hacker initialized. Stage lights overhead beamed bright as Max stood at the podium, ready to announce this year's Woodwest Middle School winner for Worst Teacher of the Year. On the dais across from Max sat a reluctant Mr. North, who, frankly, didn't look much like he wanted to be there. (In fact, he didn't, and twice he had tried to wake up from the dream only to be knocked back into slumber by the Dream Hacker.)

"Our next prize is awarded to that individual who has achieved the esteemed status of Worst Teacher of the Year," Max announced. "In a world where bad teaching is, sadly, a norm that plagues our school system and cheats our young people of the education they deserve, one would think that adjudicating a contest for the candidate most deserving of this auspicious award might be difficult. Not this year at Woodwest Middle School! Taking into account our nominee's egregious teaching policies, extraordinary lack of fairness, and overall poor conduct, the vote this year was unanimous and uncontested." Max reached for a trophy on the table behind his lectern. Its crown was an actual bust of Mr. North, and at the base, engraved with gold lettering, were Mr. North's favorite words as Max saw it: *Deeply Disappointed.*

"And now, let's hear a round of applause for this year's winner: Mr. Seymour J. North!"

In Max's mind, what was to happen next in this dream was that Mr. North would just take his trophy, offer a half smile to the audience and the cameras, and then shrink back into his seat. But Mr. North didn't even reach for the trophy or acknowledge the existence of the audience when he walked up to the dais. Instead, he placed his hand gently on Max's back and whispered softly. "Max, is all of this because I gave you a poor grade on your dystopian narrative?"

Max was not expecting Mr. North to put up a fight or to bring actual facts to the fore. "It was unanimous," Max repeated. "Now take your stupid trophy!"

"Max, the work *was* sloppy, and I know you can do better. How would you have graded it?"

Max's face flushed with anger. "You should never have assigned it! You give me all this extra work for nothing, and I'm done with it!"

Mr. North stepped back. "I thought you liked the extra challenge, Max. Why didn't you say something?"

"Yeah, right. Since when does complaining about workload do anything? You don't care!"

"Actually, I do care, Max." Mr. North thought for a moment and looked down. "You're right. I really can't expect that you would feel comfortable enough to come complaining to me. I'm sorry. I should have been more careful with assigning extra work, and I certainly could have been a lot more supportive of you, and maybe others, too."

On that note, the last of the Dream Steam pulsed through the meter, and the scene faded.

Maybe Mr. North isn't such a bad guy after all, Max thought to himself as the Orb dispensed a final dose of euphoria and melted from view.

CHAPTER 19

Max spent Sunday out with his mom, who had a rare day off from work. She had saved $150 of tips on a debit card for the two of them to spend on some much-needed shopping and food for dinner. So, after hitting the outlets and catching a free outdoor concert in town, Max grabbed the card and picked up some burgers for grilling. All was well, but by nightfall, as the coals began to glow, Max could already sense the waning of the prior day's Orb and felt a palpable and growing thirst for another Orb as soon as possible.

Of course, his mom noticed immediately. "You're looking down, Max. Is there anything I can get you?"

Max wasn't about to tell his mom about the Orb, so he drummed up the next-best excuse—one that would surely satisfy his mom. "Yeah, actually, yes, Mom. I'd kind of like to know what you meant by Dad not really leaving."

His mom sighed. "I don't know what to tell you, Maxy. He left because he had to go. I can't explain it to you now."

"Why can't you? I'm old enough to know what happened." Max stood his ground, mostly out of sheer annoyance at not having been told the truth. "You told me he left, and then that he didn't leave, and now, he left again. What's going on, Mom?"

"I made him leave, Max. I can't tell you more until you're older."

Max took a step back. "Oh. That's OK, Mom. When I'm older." He already knew where his next dream hacking adventure would take him.

CHAPTER 20

Max awoke that evening to a sphere that contained an unusual array of beautiful colors. There were the common bands of blues and greens, but in this Orb, each stripe was intertwined with gorgeous orange and yellow lacing accompanied by equally alluring crimson-red puffs that gradually became more pronounced and striking. As it matured, it floated weightlessly to the ceiling, migrating in slow circles. Max shot a glance to the window to make sure it was open and then watched with glee as the Orb drifted toward him. When it was finally within reach, Max took a deep breath, closed his eyes in expectation of the moment of entry, and gently touched his nose to the sphere.

The Orb took immediate notice of Max's presence and swiftly encased him in its warmth. Max held tight to the chair as throbs of light splashed around him like fireworks.

The new, warmer shades of colors seemed to bring with them echoes of distant purring which turned to song, and soon he could discern a sound like a hundred pixies chanting hymns in unison. There was silence, and then the choir began to sing.

> *My Orbs illuminate the world*
> *In blue and spiral whorls*
> *An awesome feat, serene and sweet,*
> *My choir sings in chorals.*
>
> *I dream in REM the thoughts of men*
> *And women while they slumber.*
> *And play while they display their deepest*
> *Feelings unencumbered.*

Max's attention grew deeper as the illuminated spirals wrapped around his periphery in harmony with the music, and he listened as the concert continued.

> *My mist ascends above me,*
> *In fancy weaves and lacing.*
> *My threads delight the unsuspecting,*
> *Ready for embracing.*

As the choir sang, the strands of yellow and orange lacing tightened around the blue and green bands and swallowed them up. The new array of colors, which resembled a hazy sunset, were unlike any the Orb had produced before, and the choir opened to the next stanza.

To those deserving of my cause,
I spin a lamp of silk.
Illuminated bright and clear,
Intended for that ilk,
Not here.

The intensity of the choir heightened as the colors darkened and the haze turned opaque. The crimson-red puffs exploded into pellets of fire, and Max's skin turned warm. Too warm. Yet the choir continued, as it apparently had more to say.

Thieving and deceiving. My
Bands turn shades of orange.
Anger swells inside me
with the charlatan beside me.
Swine and guttersnipe, he derides me,
Desk with chair he climbs me.
To take that which belongs to meeee.
He lies, he lies, he lies…

Just then, all of the orange and yellow lacing collapsed toward him and burst into flames, and Max felt the sensation of sweltering heat scorching his skin like desert sand as smothered pellets of fire rained on him while at the same time showering the air with the sordid scent of burnt cigar.

Losing his balance on the chair, Max plunged to the floor, hitting his hip against the edge of the desk as he took the fall. As he lay on the floor in agony, the fading sound of laughter and derision could be heard in the distance.

Max scampered to his bed and lay there, aching horribly, worried that his mom would wake up from all the clamor. When all remained quiet, though, Max relaxed enough to reflect on what had happened. Naturally, he was furious at the Box for tricking him, but deep inside he knew that at least part of the fault was his for using the Box's Orbs without permission. On the other hand, he reckoned, the Box didn't have to do that to him just to be mean.

Max devised a believable excuse for his mom and stayed home from school the next day. Everything ached, even his tongue, which he had bitten when he took the tumble. But the worst part was the gnawing, nagging desire for another Orb. It was as though his body was on fire and didn't know what to do with itself. He lay in bed shaking, confused, and scared, his heart beating palpably like a snare drum, and his mind screaming, shouting, begging for one thing—another Orb.

By nightfall, Max couldn't bear it any longer. He needed an Orb no matter what it would take, even if that meant swallowing his pride. He approached the Box, his voice shallow.

"Please make me an Orb."

The Box chuckled. "Why don't you just steal one like you've been doing?"

"You know why. I'm sorry. Please give me an Orb. I need one."

The Box purred. "My offer stands," it said. "You share

your intellectual prowess with me, and I will share my Orbs with you."

"What if I change my mind and want my 'intellectual prowess' back?" Max asked.

"You should be able to get most of it back," the Box said, "that is, should you decide you don't want my Orbs anymore."

"Are you including Dream Hacker in the deal?"

The Box scoffed. "Fashioning Dream Steam is difficult and time-consuming. However, in the interest of this business deal, I will add it when I can. No promises."

Max acquiesced and, as instructed, prompted the transition by holding the Box firm to his forehead and declaring his agreement to the Box's demand. There were no bolts of lightning or audible swooshes to mark the event, and Max simply put the Box back down and the deal was done.

CHAPTER 21

Relations between Max and the Box recovered immediately. The Box went out of its way to treat Max kindly and was generous not only with its Orbs but in helping with homework, giving advice, and being a true confidant and friend. In fact, as long as it wasn't offended or didn't happen to be in a bad mood, Max learned, the Box was the best friend a person could ever have. It was fun, chatty, and full of exciting ideas, dreams, and aspirations. The Orbs it produced were better and more satisfying than ever, and Max went to school each day more than happy with the arrangement.

It took several days before Max encountered another Orb equipped with Dream Steam and a Dream Hacker dashboard. When the opportunity finally arose, Max was ready. His mom would be his next target. Surely, it was within his rights to know what had happened to his father. The "Setting" command would come in handy, Max figured.

"Dream Hacker is now ready. Name your target," the voice said.

"Target, my mom, Setting," Max declared.

As a small stream of mist flowed from the cloud over Max's head to the SETTING indicator, the voice prompted Max for permission to access and retrieve a mind-print, which Max readily allowed. After the countdown from five, as Dream Hacker initialized, a flurry of mist cast heavy brush strokes upon the surface of the Orb, evoking the setting and vicissitudes of Max's father's departure. Though drawing in part from Max's own mind-print, Dream Hacker also borrowed heavily from experiences buried deep within his mother's subconscious—memories that Max would have had no way of recalling himself.

Soon the full scene emerged. Against the wall stood a tall, mahogany grandfather clock, its gears still rustily marking time, its face a sentinel keeping watch over a large living room. At a small table, Max's mother pored over bank invoices and statements while Max's father punched keys on his computer.

"It doesn't make sense, Stan. The credit card should have been paid directly by bank deposit. What does it show on your computer?"

"The balance is definitely low, but a lot of that is because of the money George borrowed, and I should be getting it back any day now."

"Last month, it was Charlie's new investment, Stan. And now George?"

Stan looked down. "I'll take care of it, Gin; don't you worry."

And with a flurry of mist, the scene morphed to the outdoors of a large two-story house as a car pulled forward hurriedly into the driveway.

"C'mon, dear." Max watched as his mom unbuckled a younger version of himself from the back seat and headed into the house. "Stan, where are you?"

Stan looked up from the paper. "What is it, honey?"

"My savings account! I went to draw funds for that lovely chaise lounge we talked about getting, and the teller said we already made our three maximum withdrawals for the month. You didn't pull from my savings, did you?"

"Oh, yours? I have to check, hon. Might have taken some out temporarily."

In another flurry of mist, the scene transformed again, this time confirming in Max's mind what might have happened when he was just a toddler.

"Stan, I want you to meet Loreli." A tall woman in slacks and a jacket smiled, gesturing pleasantly to Stan. "She's a private investigator, and she's helping me understand where our money has gone."

Max's father's face flushed. "I told you why the balance is low right now, and I didn't agree to an investigator!" Stan scowled, but Max could tell that his father was scared.

Gin glared back at him. "I didn't agree to you withdrawing my inheritance money or taking a second mortgage on this house, which I paid for." She turned to Loreli, who had gathered documents from her attaché. "She'll show you what I mean."

Loreli handed Stan a packet of receipts and other documents. "Those on top," she explained, "are copies of ATM receipts from a casino in Uptown. We have plenty of evidence—photos of you there, interviews with casino employees who claim to know you, copies of loan papers…it's all included."

Stan thumbed through the documents, his demeanor defiant. "It's not illegal to be at a casino!" he yelled.

"True," the woman said softly, "but you obtained funds by forging your wife's signature and wiping out her personal savings, and that *is* illegal."

The scene then faded, and Max glanced despondently at the now-empty meter. *My father is a crook, and he took all of our money! We had a house! We had savings! We were a family! Why did he gamble it all away? Why did he gamble* me *away?*

The Orb dissipated, but not before wrapping Max in a warm blanket of serenity that was almost, but not quite, strong enough to mask the hard emotions welling inside of him over the revelations regarding his father.

After a night's sleep, the matter still weighed heavily on him. So, on the way to school, he confided in Emile, the only friend he had who had ever met his father.

"Emy, do you remember my father at all?"

"Not really, Max, it was a long time ago, though my dad

sometimes jokes about when your dad threw me in the air and dropped me. He says that's why I have trouble in school. He says, 'imagine if Einstein had been dropped on his head as a kid.' Why do you ask?"

"Well, my mom told me that he didn't just leave."

"What, he's still around?!"

"No, he left, but there's more to the story. She didn't say exactly."

"Well, my parents have never said anything to me. I mean, your dad moved out the first month you came to our neighborhood. What does your mom say?"

"She won't say. Not until I'm older. But I kind of have an idea." Max wiped a tear with the back of his hand. If there was anyone he would tell, it would be Emy. "He might have taken money from…someone."

"You mean like a criminal? Is he in jail?"

"That's what I'm trying to find out. Don't say anything about this to anyone, whatever you do! My mom doesn't know I know."

CHAPTER 22

Though the Orbs had apparently cost Max his "intellectual prowess," Max didn't really notice any change. Of course, that might have been because his classes were not very challenging to begin with.

The only minor difference was in Mr. North's class. During a presentation on theme in *The Giver*, for example, Max's answer to a class question elicited, for the first time ever, a "could be" response from Mr. North. ("Could be" and "That's an interesting idea" were Mr. North's ways of saying that a student's answer was stupid or wrong without actually saying that the student's answer was stupid or wrong.) Though Swagger and some of the other kids still copied from Max, that was only because the Box was helping Max with the answers or because the questions were too easy. In any case, Max had found that the easiest way to navigate class was to keep quiet and only answer questions when he had to.

Mr. North did specifically ask Max to help Swagger catch up on the week's classroom assignments, though. Swagger had been sent home for two days, suspended after multiple warnings from Mr. North to stop insulting other students. The final straw was when Mustache walked into class from a hard workout in PE, apparently without showering. In doing so, she invariably conjured a toxic odor that quickly permeated the classroom in a blanket of noxious fumes, prompting hoots and howls from the class. Swagger, demonstrating his budding acting ability, performed a live choking scene, holding his hands over his nose and mouth and gagging desperately for air. Prostrating himself on the ground in sheer despair, he was just at the point of death by asphyxiation when Mustache broke out crying and two other girls took her side in pity. Swagger was pinned for the crime, and he disappeared for the rest of the day and the next.

CHAPTER 23

That afternoon, Max unburdened himself to the Box. Besides the extra work from Mr. North, he explained, class was boring without Swagger. With great interest, the Box listened to every detail about Swagger's suspension and Mustache's social difficulties.

The next day, when Max got home from school, the Box seemed rather agitated; it clearly had something on its mind and had not yet even begun spinning its next Orb. Max asked the Box if everything was OK, but the Box was quiet and just vibrated, so he waited for an answer.

"I'm troubled, boy," the Box commented. "There's something that I need."

Max listened intently. "Sure, what is it?"

"I need a pocket mirror," said the Box. "But not just any pocket mirror—a quality pocket mirror. A really good pocket mirror."

Max gave it some thought. "The only really good one I know is my mom's. She got it from her grandmother."

"That's perfect!" the Box said. "Bring it to me. I need it."

Max thought again. "Well, um, you can't, um, have that mirror. It's my mom's, and it means a lot to her."

The Box vibrated ominously.

Max did not want to offend the Box because he really needed an Orb. "Um. Can I get you a *different* mirror?"

"No!" the Box exploded. "Why won't you bring me *that* mirror?"

"Because it's not mine!" Max said, his voice rising.

The Box glowered. "Since when do you care about something being *yours*? You took the bicycle and stole my Orbs!"

Max was about to argue, but he refrained. Instead, he directed his attention on a solution, desperate for one that would mollify the angry Box.

"What if I just lend the mirror to you?" Max suggested. "Would you give it back when you're done?"

The Box thought for a moment. "Of course," it said softly. "If you want the mirror back after I have finished with it, you may certainly have it."

Relieved, Max hurried to his mom's bedroom closet, where he hastily unloaded her old keepsakes from storage boxes on the upper shelves in search of the mirror. It took a while, but eventually he found it. Unwrapping the mirror carefully from a packing cloth, Max admired the piece, caressing the embroidered casing that his great-grandmother had sewn onto the mirror generations earlier.

Max put all the things back in the boxes as they had been

and brought the mirror to his room, putting it on his desk and then placing the Box on top of it. The Box was deeply impressed with the mirror and purred happily.

"You've done a very good job, boy!" it said. "Now, if you don't mind, turn the lights out."

Max was not pleased with the idea of turning out the lights, but he did as he was instructed. What followed was a loud cracking sound as a massive bolt of light shot out from the Box and the mirror.

Max fell to the floor. "Are you OK?" he called out. "What happened? Can I turn the lights back on?"

"We are fine!" the Box said softly.

Not so reassured, Max got up and turned on the switch, but when he retrieved the mirror, he discovered, to his horror, that its beautifully embroidered fabric had been burned to a crisp and was now as black as coal. Max tried hopelessly to brush off the ash, but it felt as hot as fire. Even if it had been cool to the touch, he could tell that the embroidery had completely disintegrated. His great grandmother's embroidery was gone, and he was to blame. The awful realization struck hard. *I'm a thief, just like my father.*

"You ruined my mom's mirror!" Max cried. "She'll throw me out when she finds it missing!"

"I have made your mirror so much better," the Box declared proudly. "But your work is not done, boy." The Box purred. "Tomorrow at school, you are to deliver this mirror to the girl you call Mustache. You will have your next Orb *only* after you have done my will."

Max melted into his chair. He didn't know what the Box was up to, but it had to be something bad. He'd chuck the mirror on the way to school, he decided. And he'd tell the Box he gave it to her.

As if reading his mind, the Box added ominously, "And don't you dare lie to me, boy. I will know for myself whether you have done my bidding or not."

Max buried his head in his arms. It was no use trying to quell the trembling—besides being in panic mode, Max's body was also letting him know that the prior Orb was wearing off and that he would be needing another one sooner or later.

"What about my Orb?" Max whispered, resigned to probably being refused.

The Box vibrated quietly for a few minutes. "I will spin a small Orb for you tonight. No Dream Steam, though," the Box said, "and on the condition that you assure me the deed will be done without delay." The Box purred. "Of course, tomorrow's Orb will more than make up for what you don't get today."

Ashamed of himself and dejected, but at the same time realizing he had no choice, Max reluctantly submitted to the Box's demands. That evening, he touched his nose to the small Orb offered to him, happy with the relief it provided, and fell into a deep sleep.

CHAPTER 24

The next day, after planning how to best get the mirror to Mustache, Max settled on dropping it surreptitiously into her purse when she wasn't looking. This, he figured, would best be achieved in Mr. North's class, where she sat in the last row and closest to the door. Any excuse to leave the classroom was a potential opportunity to deliver the mirror. Max's problem was that in two years of North, he had never once requested to get up from his seat, so even a bathroom visit could elicit suspicion. Then there was the additional problem of accessing Mustache's purse at a time when she wouldn't be watching it. Mustache often took a hall pass during class, but Max couldn't remember whether she customarily took her purse with her when leaving the classroom or not.

North played a video for the first twenty minutes of class, so everyone stayed put. Once the video ended, though, students moved around more, and Mustache raised her hand to be excused. Max watched for an opening to make his move, but hope faded when she turned back toward her seat to grab her purse on the way out.

Mustache returned about ten minutes later, but by then, Max held little hope of delivering the mirror to her or getting his Orb that evening. So it was a welcome surprise when she asked to leave again, this time for a drink, *without* her purse. In a stroke of sheer genius, Max promptly shot his hand into the air, held his other hand to his mouth, and garbled loudly, "I'm gonna throw up." Naturally, he was given a green light to leave class, and he "stumbled" his way down Mustache's aisle, holding on to desks for support while doing some impressively realistic fake gagging along the way. All it took was some strategic coughing over Mustache's desk to muffle the sound of a pocket mirror dropping into her purse, and the deed was done.

CHAPTER 25

When Max got home from school, he noticed an odd, staticky noise in his room that sounded a lot like an antique radio tuner. He assumed it was something to do with the Box, so he drew nearer and listened.

"Hey, Box, what's with the noise?"

The Box was busy, or napping, and didn't immediately respond, so Max waited there, monitoring the sounds coming out of its middle. He could hear voices in the distance, and the occasional slamming door, but no discernable conversations.

The Box had, in fact, been taking a snooze, but as soon as it woke up, it cut out the radio sound and greeted Max with a hero's welcome.

"Well done, boy!" The Box was beside itself with joy. "I am spinning a wonderful Orb for you. Tonight, you shall have it in celebration of Baby!"

"Huh?" Max raised an eyebrow. "Baby?"

"Baby is already serving Mustache with great distinc-tion!" the Box said.

Max didn't know what the Box meant by that, but he cer-tainly didn't want to dampen the Box's enthusiasm in any way by saying the wrong thing. So, when his mom got home, he left the Box alone to work on his Orb and went out to spend some time with her. She was occupied, though, shuf-fling through cabinets, apparently in search of something.

"Uh, Mom? What'cha looking for?"

"Oh, Max! Sorry for not saying hi. I'm missing some-thing really important. It's small, about the size of my hand, like a booklet."

Max's heart skipped three beats, fleeing to his toes for cover. "Oh, um. What's missing, exactly?" He tried to ap-pear calm as he shuffled piles, looking for whatever she was.

"I thought it was in my purse. A small booklet with some food stamps. I needed them at the grocery. Mr. Barnes let me take the cart, though. Said I can pay him later."

"The food stamps?" Max said, his heart stumbling its way back to his chest. "Is that what you're missing?"

"You've seen 'em?"

"Yeah," Max said. He pulled a small plastic wallet from a pile of clipped store coupons. "You left them with these."

"Oh, Maxy. I don't know what I'd do without you. I was going crazy looking." She dropped onto the sofa.

"Mom, have we always struggled for money like this?"

"Uh, why do you ask?"

"Just wondering, um, if our being poor has anything to do with my father. I'm thinking maybe…well, maybe he took our money?"

Max watched his mother closely as she squirmed uncomfortably in her seat and fell silent.

"Well, did he?" Max repeated.

"Max, he didn't *steal* anything; he *squandered* it on gambling. Reckless gambling. He would borrow money, thinking that he would pay it back with the winnings, but there were rarely any winnings. He ate through our accounts, and more. Even after we sold our furniture and moved here, he still couldn't stop himself, and he wouldn't get help either. I had to tell him to leave."

Max thought about the mirror he had "borrowed" and looked down. "Where is Dad now?"

"I don't know. Haven't seen him in years."

CHAPTER 26

That night, the Orb was everything the Box had said it would be. It contained a new element too—glitter. Millions of shiny specks of glitter swirled about the Orb like a snow globe, arranging themselves like pixels drawing pictures of people and objects. The images, alive and animate, swelled in all three dimensions to form figures as if in a cartoon. It was like watching live Looney Tunes, but the characters looked more real than on TV. They were exciting to look at too, but for Max, the best thing was that they got his mind off thinking about his father. Even after the Orb evaporated, the glitter remained, continuing to conjure vibrant, animated figures that danced vivaciously before Max's eyes.

At school the next day, Max tried his best to tune in to what was going on in class, but he found that the Mind Glitter characters were so much more exciting to watch than classes were, so even when teachers covered really interesting subjects that Max had enjoyed in the past, the information they presented was dull in comparison to the hallucinated animated creatures gallivanting around him. As his glitterated eyes scanned the classroom, a waddle of pixeled penguins could be seen puttering up and down the aisles and climbing into the cubbies at the back of the room. On Adrienne's lap, Max spotted a tortoise resting comfortably, while several goldfish sat playing cards together on a high windowsill with their fins hanging from the ledge. A larger-than-usual spider dangled from the radiator against the wall, but Max wasn't quite sure if the arachnid was real or just a vision caused by the glitter. At the back of the room, Mustache sat in her seat staring at her new pocket mirror and making faces. She had shaved off the hairs over her lip, though only Max had realized this, as evidenced by the fact that none of his classmates had yet started rumors. Her seat, Max noticed, was about the only place he could find that was not obstructed by glitter-animated creatures. Even his own hallucinations seemed to avoid her.

When Max got home, the Box was still ecstatic over Baby and promised to spin a "very nice" Orb for Max that evening. By that time, the Mind Glitter had worn off, and he was eager for more.

"I was hoping there would be some more of that Mind Glitter in my Orb tonight?" Max petitioned as nonchalantly as possible.

The Box purred. "According to our agreement, I am to

provide you with Orbs including Dream Steam periodically. Concocting Mind Glitter is a completely different story, however, which requires extremely laborious effort on my part. If you want my Mind Glitter, you will need to make a trade."

"Then why did you give it to me free last night?"

"It was just a gift sample for your edification. Pharmaceutical companies give samples all the time; why shouldn't I?"

Max made a note to look up the word "edification," though the idea of another trade with the Box did not sit well with Max, whatever the word meant. "What exactly did you have in mind for me to give you?"

"Ahh, well, I certainly would agree to have some of your *serenity* for it," the Box replied. "After all, you have little need for *serenity* when you can have *euphoria* from my Mind Glitter instead."

While Max recalled learning those words in school, he had never heard them used in normal conversation. *Serenity* meant a feeling of calm while *euphoria*'s definition was a feeling of intense happiness, and Max wasn't sure if it was such a good idea to give away the attribute of calmness, even for something seemingly wonderful like euphoria. Moreover, after already having lost some of his intellectual prowess to the Box—not that he could really feel the difference—Max was reticent to make yet another trade with it.

"I'll pass on the Mind Glitter for now."

"Your loss," the Box replied coldly.

CHAPTER 27

Without the Mind Glitter to distract him, Max's disposition turned sullen. He obsessed constantly over his father's misdeeds and whereabouts, and he worried that his own conduct was somehow tied to that of his progenitor, and that he was doomed to come to the same end. One thing that was clear was that he needed to know more about his missing father, to find out what had happened to him after he moved out and where he might be now. So, when the mist in that evening's Orb lifted to reveal the Dream Hacker dashboard, Max knew just who he wanted to target.

"Dream Hacker is now ready. Name your target," the voice said.

"Target my father!" Max declared softly.

As the familiar thin current of steam drifted from the cloud over Max's head to the dashboard, Max noticed a significant dip in the meter level, but even so, the chamber remained grey. *Maybe he's just not sleeping right now.* Max was about to try the Setting command but stopped short as the dashboard's voice signaled that his time was up. Sure enough, the meter indicated empty, and indeed, the steam was gone. *Why did it use up my time if there was no dream?* Max wondered.

As much as Max tried over the coming days to bury his worries and concerns about his father and about his own identity, nothing provided him with the relief he had experienced with the Mind Glitter. Yet his requests for more went nowhere.

"I won't give you any Mind Glitter unless you make a trade," the Box repeated after multiple entreaties from Max.

"I need it!" Max implored. Max knew there was no point in pretending. He was miserable in school, bitter at home, and considered himself at fault for all his problems.

He held out for a week, but finally Max succumbed and agreed to the Box's terms. Max was instructed to carry the Box wherever he went, including bringing it to school hidden in his pocket so that he could get a second dose of the glitter at school, if he needed it, by reaching into his pocket and rubbing the Box gently with the back of his hand.

CHAPTER 28

Max and the Box enjoyed an amicable relationship over the next several weeks. The Box, true to its word, furnished Max with incredibly beautiful Orbs amply sprinkled with generous quantities of Mind Glitter, along with Dream Steam on occasion. The Box also produced perfect pre-copies of two important exams for Max to cheat on, and helped Max get through his homework to a basic standard (which wasn't much). As for Max, his life revolved almost entirely around the Orbs, the Mind Glitter, to some extent the Dream Steam, and, especially, on not upsetting the Box.

The Box had a temper, Max knew. And it did not always respond to reason, especially when it wanted something that Max could not easily deliver. This had been the case with his mom's mirror and, to Max's chagrin, would soon be the case again. Sure enough, the Box had another job for Max to do.

"Max, I need you to get me an elegant glass serving dish

right away," the Box said. "Something Italian, like Bacca-rat, might be especially nice."

"Oh man, you're not making another magic mirror, are you?" Max sniggered.

The Box hummed in agreement. "We need to find a *very* expensive panel of glass—it can be a dish or a display plate, but it must be rectangular, procured only from a *very* elite establishment," the Box declared. "We shall steal it this weekend."

"Huh?" Max gulped. "You mean—*you* shall steal it—not me!"

Max regretted replying so quickly, but he didn't know what else to say.

"I mean, I'm sure we can find you a *very* expensive dish without having to *steal* it," Max added.

What came out of the Box at that juncture was a torrent of vulgar language and vitriol the likes of which Max had never heard expressed by anyone in his life, the main thrust of which was that Max was a complete lowlife, a thief, and undeserving of the Box's benevolence.

"You are going to get me the glass *this weekend*, or else!" The Box vibrated ominously. "You wouldn't want your girl-friend, Mustache, to go telling Mr. North that you cheat on his tests, would you?"

"She's not my girlfriend," Max retorted weakly.

"For sure she's not," the Box snorted. "Who would want you anyway? You're nothing, you thief!"

Max had nothing to say or do other than curl up into a little ball as he felt his world crumbling around him. His entire life revolved around the Box and its Orbs, and it was all his fault.

Maybe the Box is right, Max thought. *I'm just a dirty, no-good, cheating thief, and now I'm going to have to go shoplift from a store to make it happy.*

The Box gave Max an Orb that day (albeit without Mind Glitter or Dream Steam), but the next day, Friday, it refused without first getting a promise that Max would steal the merchandise that weekend. After some discussion, the two decided to target Perry's Boutique, a high-end luxury-goods store downtown, about a mile and a half away. The plan was that Max would watch the entrance of the store from across the street until some random middle-aged couple arrived, appearing as if they were about to go in to shop. On cue, Max would then take a position near that couple and walk into the store as though he were their child straggling along. As they went about their business in the store, Max would wander about in search of some glassware fancy enough to satisfy the Box, and, once found, would hide it in his backpack before making a surreptitious exit. The Box, for its part, would jam the cameras when Max tapped it in his pocket.

Max's mom was off from work on Saturday, so that left Sunday to get the job done. Max tracked down an old backpack that he thought wouldn't look too suspicious in a luxury store, but when he went to put the Box in his pocket, his arms were so jittery he could hardly hold the Box without trembling.

"Stop shaking me!" the Box demanded. "I'm gonna throw up."

"I can't help it," Max said. "I'm nervous."

"Here. You better take this," the Box said.

At that moment, the Box produced a new type of Orb, colored solid purple, and prompted Max to touch it with his nose. Max followed the usual routine, but his experience with this Orb was different than the others. It was smaller, not particularly pretty, and oddly, it smelled like mint.

"I thought you didn't like the smell of mint?"

"Never mind that," the Box said. "This Orb will make you less nervous and will cancel out the Mind Glitter so you don't hallucinate policemen and get scared and run."

Sure enough, the Orb made Max feel psyched up and ready for anything, as though he hadn't a care in the world. He never knew he had such strength and ability.

"I can do anything!" Max said confidently.

"Good," the Box purred. "Let's go to the store while it lasts."

CHAPTER 29

Keeping watch over the parking lot, Max looked out for a suitable couple to shadow. First, he observed and subsequently rejected some old lady and (probably) her daughter who looked like serious customers but had parked in a fifteen-minute zone. He spotted and ruled out a woman who was by herself, carrying boxes into the store. She was probably just going to make a return, and besides, she seemed the type of person likely to notice Max tagging along at her side, even if it were just for a few moments.

Nobody approached the place for the next forty-five minutes, so Max just continued waiting. Then came a couple who looked just the right age to be Max's parents, and Max readied himself to attach onto his acquired host, but a young girl promptly popped out of the back seat just when Max thought the two adults were alone. He wasn't sure if the girl would mess things up, so he aborted that plan.

Another thirty minutes went by.

Finally, at about 4 p.m., an hour before closing, Max decided he'd better act now or never, and that he should take the best next option for hosts, even if they were not necessarily the ideal candidates. He settled on an older couple who walked into the store from a car parked at a meter on the street. Max noted that "Grandpa" fed at least three quarters into the meter, which meant they expected to be in the store for about forty-five minutes. In this scheme, Max figured he would play their grandchild.

The ruse seemed to work when they entered the premises, and Max soon found himself floating around the store on his own, perusing luxury goods, careful not to look too interested in any of the products. Max took stock of where the employees were standing and checked the walls for surveillance mirrors. He found only cameras, including one affixed behind a cash register, but the cameras were the Box's responsibility, so Max ignored them. There was a large stairway leading to a downstairs showroom, and from the top of the stairs, Max could see several fully set tables with dishes of various designs and styles on the lower floor. A saleslady sat in virtual solitude at a second cash register behind the display tables downstairs.

There were two salesladies working on the main floor, and both were helping customers, so Max got to work searching the merchandise without too much concern that he was being watched. One shelf housed a gorgeous array of glass dishes, but the entire set was oval and of no apparent use to the Box. There was a suitable piece in a wall display behind the cashier's desk, but the door to the display was shut with a sliding-window keylock that would not open without the key. Max tried.

Having exhausted all possibilities on the main floor, Max took the stairs and checked all of the display tables on the lower floor for suitable dishes. Unfortunately, every last piece except the drinking glasses was made of ceramic, not glass, and the Box had specifically said glass. There was an exquisite piece on display above the downstairs cash register that looked as though it might be perfect for the Box. It was a rectangular glass serving dish, with five short, decorative silver legs on the bottom that supported the piece and kept the bottom of the well elevated so that the glass wouldn't break if the vessel were put down on a hard surface.

Max ducked behind a nearby display cabinet to be as close to the item as possible, his hand already in his pocket, ready to tap the Box when it was time to block the camera. He lifted his head over the counter to check for salesladies—none in sight—and when the coast was clear, he tapped the Box, passed stealthily behind the counter, reached up to the shelf, snatched the merchandise, and stuffed the dish into his backpack.

Easy. Too easy, Max thought.

Max made his way back up the stairs as nonchalantly as possible. He quickly spotted the old couple who, conveniently, looked as though they were about to leave the store.

Each had bags in both arms and the husband had his car key in his hand. But as Max approached the exit to slip out with them, a saleslady came from behind carrying a large carton, which Max didn't know also belonged to the couple. Now, with this saleslady tagging along outside, he could not possibly walk with them to their car, because at some point he would be asked who he was, and that would surely give up his game. On the other hand, if he tried to just walk off now, he would likely arouse suspicion. Thinking fast, Max hatched a plan to get rid of the saleslady.

"May I help carry that to the car for you?" he asked her.

The saleslady smiled, stretching the countless wrinkles that adorned her face in every direction at once.

"Oh, how sweet!" she said. "What a *nice* boy! Here, let me take your backpack so you have both hands."

That was not going to work so well, Max thought as he frantically searched for the most helpful reply. (This saleslady was getting to be a serious pest.)

"Um. No, it's OK," Max said. "I can carry them both."

Max then reached out to take the carton from the saleslady, but when he extended his hands to take hold of the carton, the backpack with the stolen merchandise, which he had draped over his shoulder, swiveled with the rotation of his arm and smacked hard against the outside of the cardboard carton, producing a very audible clanking noise that did not go unnoticed. In the meantime, the couple loaded all their bags into their car, returned once to retrieve the carton, and then drove away, leaving Max and the saleslady on the sidewalk outside the store.

The saleslady's nose lifted suspiciously. "What do you have in that backpack, young man?" She took hold of one of the straps and gripped it tightly before Max could think to run.

"Oh, um. It's a gift for my mother," Max lied. "I bought it downstairs."

Ms. Pest looked dubious. "How did you pay for it?" she asked.

Max panicked, checking his pockets for a wallet he knew he didn't have, and, to his amazement, produced the credit card his mom had given him on their day out for lunch. *What a break! I can't believe I'm wearing the same pair of pants.* He handed the lady the credit card and prayed that she would not make him wait around while she checked with the cashier downstairs to corroborate his story.

"Where's the receipt?" she asked.

"It was emailed to my mom," Max lied. "See, it's her birthday, and I saved up all my allowance money to pay her back. I really need to go now because I told her I'd be home a half hour ago and she will worry terribly that I'm late."

The saleslady paused, still dubious, yet giving serious thought to what Max had said. After what seemed to Max like an eternity of reflection, she let him go. Max took the backpack and scurried off as quickly as he could without looking too nervous. Once out of sight, though, he scrammed out of there as fast as his legs would carry him.

CHAPTER 30

By the time Max got home, the purple Orb had all but worn off, and Max felt sick to his stomach over what he had done. The wrinkled face of the saleslady kept popping into his consciousness and telling him how nice a boy he was, only to come back a few minutes later frowning over her apparent displeasure and disappointment in him. Max took to his bed, desperately needing to relax, his head pounding from stress and his shirt soaked with sweat. The only consolation as far as Max was concerned was that his efforts should at least please the Box enough to get an Orb and some Mind Glitter to go with it.

Max pulled the Box out from his pocket and listened for snoring to make sure it wasn't asleep. Once satisfied that he wouldn't disturb the Box's slumber, he asked it what he should do with the glass dish.

"Do as you did with the mirror," the Box purred. "And don't forget to turn out the lights."

Max did as the Box said and braced for the loud crack and bolt of light that he remembered from the last time, but what followed was not as Max expected. Instead of a loud and sharp crack, Max's room echoed with the distinct and rather unpleasant sound of fingernails scratching a chalkboard. Accompanying this horrendous noise was a malodorous stench best described as that of a military field latrine.

The Box howled. "What is this, boy!? What did you get?"

"What's wrong?" Max said. "I got you just what you asked for."

"This piece of detritus is useless to me, you incompetent scumbag! It has metal on it!"

Sure enough, attached securely to the bottom of the glass were the five decorative legs made of silver plate.

"You never said anything about metal." Max sighed. "I didn't know."

"I said GLASS, you mentally incompetent cretin! G-L-A-S-S, GLASS!"

Lashing out at Max with venom, the Box proceeded to unleash a string of crude invective.

"GO BACK THERE NOW, and get me a GLASS plate WITHOUT metal," the Box demanded, "or I will put FIRE in your Orbs that will incinerate you from the insides out."

"I can't go!" Max said. "They know me over there!"

"Then take the metal off this one!"

Max grabbed his toolbox from the floor of the closet and sat down at the desk. There were five metal attachments affixed to the bottom of the serving dish, as Max had observed. Mindful that if the glass were to break in the process, he would have to go back downtown, Max worked diligently at removing each leg, one by one, meticulously making sure that he did not dent or scratch the glass in a way that might upset the Box. The four corner legs were relatively easy to remove. They were attached by small screws that came off easily with the right size screwdriver. The center leg, however, had an attitude and only gave up after a fight. Max had inadvertently stripped the top of the screw while trying to turn it and ended up having to use a sharp peg to root the piece out by force. The Box sat as audience the whole time, hurling admonitions, unsolicited advice, condemnations of disapproval, and demeaning and disparaging comments at Max each step of the way.

When the dish was ready, Max placed it under the Box and shut off the lights. A *crack* and bolt of light followed, and the Box was back to its friendly self, even apologizing to Max for "having to be so strict with him." This, it added, was for Max's own good.

That evening, the Box spun Max a most spectacular Orb infused with a generous quantity of Mind Glitter. It also asked Max to kindly deposit the glass dish at school in the wastepaper basket located in Mr. North's classroom. Max did as he was told the next morning before school.

The students in Mr. North's class were in a state of sheer uproar the next day. All had been quiet until Mustache walked through the door dressed in skinny jeans and black ankle boots. She had lost some weight but still didn't quite fit the attire. And her hair! Her hair, which had been dyed in pink fluorescent and turquoise Manic Panic, shot in every which direction, apparently gelled to permanently fight the planet's gravitational pull. Adorning her ears were ink-black spike hoops, each with angry-looking arrows protruding from them. All in all, she was a genuine work of art. The mere apparition of such a costume-adorned girl like Mustache would in itself be riot-provoking in a seventh-grade classroom, but on top of it all, she also wore a loud Candy perfume that smelled like a mix of black licorice and WD-40, an anti-rust compound sold at better hardware stores.

Naturally, Swagger was busy feigning death by asphyxiation, but more seriously, the odor triggered a full-blown asthma attack in Marco Fent, who had to be paramedically rushed to the hospital for urgent care. For her part, Mustache sat at her desk admiring various facets of her new self in the mirror that she had gotten from Max. Class came to order when Mr. North walked in, but even Mr. North struggled with the pervasive odor and eventually had to ask Mustache to wait in his office. Before leaving the classroom, though, on the pretense of bringing her homework up to Mr. North, Mustache brushed by Emile's seat, dropping a note on his desk as she departed.

After class, Max waited at the door for Emile. He finally looked into the classroom and discovered to his horror that Emile was hard at work rummaging through the wastepaper basket. He was obviously in search of something, and Max knew exactly what that "something" was. *I get it,* Max thought. *Mustache's mirror must have told her to write a note telling Emy where to find the glass…and now Emy has one of these fancy glass Box Babies too!* Shocked, angry, and disgusted by his own conduct, Max walked home alone, embarrassed, and afraid to say a word to his friend, because the Box, ensconced firmly in his pocket, would hear every word he spoke.

Torn from the inside, confused, and lost in a pool of self-pity, Max meandered home, trying the best he could to summon the courage to confront the Box over Emile. But when he got home and took the Box from his pocket, he was suddenly distracted by the sound of voices. Evidently, the Box was eavesdropping on someone's conversation. This time the entire exchange was audible and clear.

"Roxie, I've asked your parents to come in because I'm concerned about you," one voice said.

That's Mr. North talking to Mustache, Max thought.

"Mr. North, I appreciate your concern for our daughter, but I am sure we can handle this ourselves at home," another voice said.

"Mr. Buckfort, I know you can, but when the academic decline is so sudden…"

"I'll try doing better on my tests," a girl's voice cried.

"And I'll keep a closer eye on Roxie to make sure she keeps up with her work," Mr. Buckfort added softly.

Mrs. Buckfort didn't say a word.

"OK then, let's see how it goes," Mr. North said, "and we can be in touch after report cards, if necessary."

Mr. Buckfort thanked Mr. North warmly when the meeting disbanded, and Max could then hear shuffling noises such as chairs scraping against the floor, the muffled sounds of the listening mirror being put in Mustache's purse, and eventually, the footsteps of the Buckforts heading back to their car. Then came the familiar sound of car doors closing as the broadcast continued. By this point, the Box had fallen asleep and was snoring fairly loudly, but Max kept listening for more conversation. He felt personally responsible for Mustache getting the mirror, and he wanted to know exactly what the mirror was doing to her. But what happened in the Buckforts' car was beyond any reasonable person's expectations and practically blew Max off his chair.

Once the Buckforts were en route home, there was a tense silence in their car, which turned unexpectedly violent. Max listened as Mr. Buckfort exploded in rage, lashing out at Mustache but also at Mrs. Buckfort. He railed at them over everything from the wasted time of having to have this meeting today with Mr. North to Mrs. Buckfort's incompetence in child-rearing to Mustache's ugly physical appearance. He was as livid as his mouth was foul. Car horns outside suggested that Mr. Buckfort was also not paying very much attention to the road.

Max gulped hard. Sounds of slapping, punching, and crying followed as Mr. Buckfort went on for another fifteen minutes, blasting his wife and daughter with obscene, expletive-ladened filth, scorn, and derision. There was no screaming back or arguing; just whimpering. Max could not fathom how Mr. Buckfort, who had been so warm and friendly in the meeting with Mr. North just a few minutes earlier, could possibly be acting this way to his family now. And why was Mrs. Buckfort so passive in the face of this horrible and demeaning treatment? After all, Max thought, had it been him, he surely would have spoken up.

Or would he?

The reality hit Max hard. Other than the slapping and the

hitting, Mr. Buckfort's conduct, Max realized, was hardly different than the way the Box had been treating him. But the Box, Max argued, had the Orbs, the Mind Glitter, and the Dream Steam. What kind of Orbs and Mind Glitter might Mr. Buckfort have hanging over his family to force them to put up with his behavior? Max felt terrible for Mustache and resolved to be nicer to her, but he could think of nothing he could do to help. After all, the Box had him under its control, and both he and the Box knew it. A despondent Max lay in bed awaiting his next Orb, courtesy of an apparently delighted Box.

CHAPTER 32

Max kept vigil that night as he waited for his next Orb to emerge, and when it finally did, he raced to press his nose against the seducing surface. The effect was immediate—the physical and emotional release from that dreadful thirst he had felt for hours, ever since the prior Orb's effects had worn off. Max's eyes drew deep into the swirls of colored mist as tiny specks of Mind Glitter shot across the sphere like darts—a captivating spectacle so mesmerizing that when the curtain of mist finally lifted, the emergence of the Dream Hacker dashboard went unnoticed until the familiar voice sounded, and he realized it was there.

"Dream Hacker is now ready. Name your target."

Max had hardly planned who to target, but with the unsettling incident involving Mr. Buckfort weighing heavily on his mind, he had no trouble extemporizing one. "Umm. Mustache, uh, I mean, Roxie Buckfort."

Straightaway, the balmy air turned frigid as thunder

clouds gathered ominously overhead amid heavy gusts of wind. A skyline appeared at a distance, and a bleak early-evening twilight reflected against a body of water below. Towering over the water was a tall, dilapidated bridge, lonely as it was grey, and otherwise desolate but for Roxanne Buckfort, who stood, unmoving, with her arms and knees folded between the rails guarding the overlook, her eyes cold and glassy and her face exhausted. *She looks miserable*, Max thought. *I should really tell her everything's going to be OK.*

Max turned toward the Dream Hacker dashboard. The meter read half full. "Hack as self," he called, and at once, he became an active and visible part of her dream.

"How did *you* get here? Is that you? Max?" Rain dripped from her face as she spoke.

"I just came to see how you're doing," he said, "because I saw what happened in the car today."

The girl turned back toward the water and stared vacantly into the void. "Leave me alone. Go."

"What about your mom?"

"What about her? She takes his side; says I get him mad and that he's OK most of the time. Well, he's not. Now, get lost!" She paced away and crossed to the opposite side of the bridge.

Max followed. "Maybe you could run away?"

"Yeah, like where he won't find me? You don't know how it is. Now, leave!!"

"Alright, I'll go. But if you need anything, tell me."

Max turned and walked away and didn't look back until the meter had emptied. He found some small comfort in knowing he had reached out to help Roxanne Buckfort, and only wished that someone would reach out to help him.

CHAPTER 33

At school the next day, Max found it difficult to concentrate because of the residual Mind Glitter. The Box had been so generous with the amount of it provided by the Orb that through most of the day, Max's field of vision was completely inundated with animated sham-creatures, figures, and objects all vying for his attention. The animations were so lifelike that during history, Max confused Mrs. Pinkston for a very realistic-looking brontosaurus. He only realized his mistake after seeing smoke coming out of her ears. Copying the equations for his math homework was made nearly impossible by a battalion of *Star Wars* storm troopers who were blocking the whiteboard. As much as Max tried getting them to move, they just raised their weapons and blocked his view even more. Even his reading assignments were confusing, because the words would suddenly start crawling around the page or exploding into thin air. In fact, with the Mind Glitter, there was never a dull moment in class—something exciting was *always* happening. The only pause button was to look back toward where Mustache sat, because the glitter always seemed to avoid her.

When Max glanced back toward her, she looked up from her mirror, and Max smiled weakly, trying to be as friendly as possible without capturing the attention and consternation of his classroom peers. He noticed that she had lost weight, and that her face looked pale. Though he hardly saw her at school between classes, he happened to run into her in the hall that day and managed to summon up the courage to let her know that he really did care.

"I meant what I said last night," he whispered.

It took her a moment to figure out what he meant by that comment, but as she recalled her dream and then realized that Max was apparently referring to it, her eyes widened in alarm, and she quickly turned away and walked in the other direction.

CHAPTER 34

Max and Emile walked home together that afternoon as usual, but they said very little to each other on the way. Max's distraction with the Box had already cut into his relationship with Emile, and the two boys had been speaking even less ever since Emy discovered the glass. Emile seemed just too tired to think and could hardly keep his eyes open. Max desperately wanted to ask him about the glass dish, but was afraid to say a word knowing that the Box would be listening to everything he said from its place in his pocket.

The fact was, Emile had changed ever since he got that glass. In the four years that Max had known Emile, he almost never missed school and certainly didn't show up late to class, as he was now prone to do. Academically, Emile had gone from being vibrant and engaged to lazily dragging from one classroom to the next, typically falling asleep at his desk while his teachers were teaching. Yet there was nothing Max could do. Emile was unreachable by phone, and discussion on the way home was not possible because of the potential for repercussions from the Box. Max even tried to hack Emile's dreams, but the Orb always came back with an error message. Error#141b, it said. Subject not sleeping.

This went on for three weeks.

Then, like night and day, Emile showed up to school after a long weekend, completely back to his old self. Granted, he was totally behind in his work, but his demeanor was normal, and he was back to being active and awake just as he had been before retrieving the glass dish from the classroom wastebasket a month earlier.

Max was hungry for an Orb with plenty of Mind Glitter that afternoon, so he resigned himself to not discussing the glass dish with Emile. But on the way home from school, Emile wanted to talk, and there wasn't too much Max could do to stop his friend from sharing what had happened to him without angering the Box, which at that point was vibrating eagerly in Max's pocket in its desire to hear what Emile was about to say.

"Max, I've never lied to you, ever, right?"

"Yeah, Emy," Max said. "What's going on?"

"It's a long story, so I'm just going to say it, whether you believe me or not. Here it goes, ready? This is what happened, and you have to believe me, OK?"

"OK, Emy. What happened?"

Emy pulled out a piece of paper from his pocket.

"I found this note on my desk like a month ago telling me that there was this very special glass thing for me in the trashcan, from someone saying they were my 'secret admirer.' This was like a month ago. I don't *have* any secret admirers, but anyway, after class, I go and find this glass dish, which I'm not sure what to do with, so I bring it home. Then I'm looking at this thing, and kind of looking through it, because it's clear and you can see through it, and I'm checking out my room through it, but you really can't see normally because it's not perfectly clear to see through. And, as I'm looking, all of a sudden there's this dragon I'm seeing there on the other side of the glass, and there's grass and trees and stuff over there too, around this dragon, and it was a fire-breathing dragon, for real, that's puffing out real fire, and not just pretend fire but real fire. It was next to me in the glass because I was holding the glass, and I could feel the hot breath of it on me, so I jerked my arms away and now I was seeing a different view through the glass. This time, I saw a big castle from the Middle Ages, like the castles Mr. Plotkin showed us last year in history. It was massive and there were these knights riding outside and this one guy walks right up to me but doesn't see me the way I see him, so he ignores me because I'm not really there or because he doesn't see through the glass from that side. So I'm in my room holding this glass and I start walking, and as I walk, when I look into the glass, it's like I'm walking over there too, so I walk toward the castle, still looking into the glass to see where I'm going. And I get to a gate about so-high up to my neck, and I can't pass the gate because it's closed with a hook that was latched shut, and I couldn't climb it because I wasn't there on that side of the glass. So I get this idea and I climb up onto my bed to get high enough, holding the glass so that in the glass I was higher up against the fence. Then I jumped as high and as far as I could off the bed and landed and looked at the glass, and sure enough, I had jumped the fence. But then I hear this loud barking, really loud, mad barking, and the sound was coming closer, and I wanted to get back outside the gate, but my bed wasn't in the right place where I was now standing, so I couldn't get myself high enough to jump over the gate again. And the dogs kept coming closer. I couldn't see them, but I sure could hear them, and I didn't know what to do. There was no time to look for an open gate, so I got back to where the latch was, and…and, I reached my hand into the glass, and my hand went through it and was *inside* the glass where the fence was, so I grabbed onto the latch and pulled it open and went out before the gate slammed shut. Just then, the dogs came— I never saw such vicious dogs—and I backed away and the dogs came rushing at the gate and were barking like crazy.

"That's when my mom called me down for dinner. So, I'm like, OK, dinner. I put the glass down and I go and wash in the bathroom to try to get rid of my sweat and get my heart to stop pounding, because it was pounding like crazy.

"We have dinner, and I'm, like, trying to play it cool and

my parents are asking me all these questions because they know me, and they know when something is up. But I made excuses and right after dinner, ran back to my room and took out the glass again, but this time there was just a message."

"What did it say? Did it talk to you?"

"No talking. The glass was like a screen. It just said to read these 'disclaimer' things and then press the button that says 'I agree.' There was all this small print to read, but the important parts in bold said that I had to agree not to tell anyone about what the glass could do, and if I did tell, it would never work for me again. I wasn't sure if I would say anything or not to my parents, but I pressed the agree button anyway, and the screen told me how to get from 'Observer' mode to 'Immersive' where the real game is played. I chose to play, and a message popped up saying my game was queuing and wouldn't start until midnight. So that's what I did—I waited for midnight."

"OK, then what happened??"

"I'm getting there! So I wait up until midnight and I'm watching the glass to see what happens, and then at midnight—well, my clock said 11:58 p.m. but it's slow, so it must have been midnight—and the glass lights up and a message says, 'Wear me like a hat.' That's all it said—'Wear me like a hat.' So I was looking and trying to figure out what that's supposed to mean, and afraid that I'm not gonna be able to get it to work, and it comes up with a new message that says, 'Are you having trouble playing the game? Press here.'

"So I pressed, and then there's this cartoon picture of a person lifting a glass, which says on it 'DISH,' and then putting it on his head. Well, I'm no dummy, so I figured out that I'm supposed to put the glass dish on my head, like a hat! So I lift it over my head, and I'm pinching the glass with my fingers tight so it won't fall and break, and I put it on top of my head like a hat, and as it touches my hair, the glass melts away in my fingers and becomes cloth like a hat, and this bright light comes down like in a circle from the hat on all sides of me, and as this light reaches my belt and then down to my shoes, I'm suddenly dressed in this really real-looking costume, and I've got a bow and arrows, and I'm in a forest, and this guy who calls himself Sir Lance comes over and tells me what I have to do and gives me Training Powder so I'll know how to work the bow. He says he'll be with me every step of the game and that I have to save the princess before morning! He says if I need to stop playing, take off the hat, but hold it tight so it doesn't fall when it turns back into glass. I can't even tell you what happened after that cuz it's such a blur, but on the third day, I actually saved a princess! I did! A real live princess! She was thirteen and really pretty. Oh, and, um, *very pleased.*"

"What happened after that, Emy?" Max said, pretending not to notice Emile's ears turning red.

"I went on adventures every night for the next week, and the week after that and then all last week. Every night, after everyone was asleep, I was off on another adventure. It was amazing!"

Now Max knew why he was never able to hack into Emy's dreams. *He was never asleep when I tried!*

"But you're telling me all about it and you weren't supposed to?"

"Yeah, I know, I broke the rule," Emile said. "I already told my parents, too. Parents may be a little weird sometimes, but they've been in the world longer than me, and mine are really smart. My parents told me a long time ago that when someone says they have something for you and *not to tell*, that usually means you *should* tell, especially if it's a stranger. I'm not sure a piece of glass is actually a stranger, but I sure don't know any 'secret admirer.'

"So I asked my dad what he would do if he had a magic glass that could play games like this, and he said he wants to live real life in the real world, not pretend stories that are fake. But he said that he would sell it on eBay for a lot of money! My mom gave him her look, you know, the one she makes when he says the wrong thing? And she told me that I wouldn't be able to stop playing and that it would ruin my life if I had it. And I thought about that a lot, because for the last three weeks, all I did was play that game all night and then sleep during the day. I would have played longer if I could. I even tried one night to tell myself that I wouldn't play so I could sleep, and I still played because I couldn't stop myself. It was just too exciting to not play."

"So what did you do about the glass?"

"Well, it was hard, Max. I knew I wasn't strong enough to handle it, so I wrapped the glass in plastic wrap, took a hammer from the garage, and smashed it into thousands of pieces. Dumped it in the trash bin outside. Now it's gone, and I miss it, but I don't really miss it. Well, I kind of do, actually."

Max had gotten so involved in Emile's story that he had completely forgotten about the Box listening to this conversation. But when Emile said the word, "smash," as in, he "smashed it into thousands of pieces," the Box went apoplectic. It burned red and gave off smoke that streamed from Max's pocket so thickly that it was a wonder Emile didn't notice. Max had a wad of tissues in his backpack, which he stuffed into his pocket between the Box and his leg so he wouldn't get burned. He was really happy for his friend, but worried about what the Box would do to him later. His respect for Emile grew that day, too. He had always considered himself smarter than his friend, but maybe not anymore. At least not when it came to making good choices. Emy was now free because he had made good choices, while he, Max, was stuck forever in a deep and ugly hole. Max thought of Emile's parents and suddenly missed the father he never knew and the mom he almost never saw.

It's not her fault, Max thought. *She has to work so we can eat.*

CHAPTER 35

Max got to his room as quickly as he could and unloaded the Box onto his desk, trying not to get his fingers scalded by the heat. He had never seen the Box looking so angry and was now in the uncomfortable position of having to ask it for an Orb. His aching muscles and clammy skin were telltale signs that his disposition over the next few hours would become miserable if he didn't get another Orb. For the sake of his condition, he decided he had better speak up. Checking first to make sure the Box wasn't sleeping, he leaned toward it saying softly, "I'm sorry about what Emile did with your Baby."

The only response from the Box was a puff of angry heat.

Max repeated, "I'm really sorry about Baby."

Same response.

Another two hours of silent treatment elapsed, but by this point, he felt nauseous and about to throw up. What could he do but beg for an Orb?

"I'm sorry about what happened, Box, but may I please have an Orb tonight?"

"You're not sorry about anything," the Box said, bristling. "You're a liar, and I hate you."

Max struggled with what to say to that because in actual fact the Box was right. He wasn't sorry, and he *was* lying just to make sure he would get an Orb.

"We will see about your friend Emile," the Box threatened. That night, it produced an Orb the likes of which Max had not seen before. "Have your Orb, boy," the Box spit. Max had never seen so many different shades of the color black as were produced in that one Orb. As the sphere formed, its surface immediately saturated with blotches of charcoal-colored and ink-black patchwork daubed with a viscous yet flowing liquified silver. The silver gravitated mostly to the top and bottom of the Orb, where it splashed back and forth like waves in a stormy sea. With every slosh, cold metal tentacles erupted from the silver ooze, each tentacle casting itself along the surface of the Orb until the entire sphere was covered in what looked from the outside like the bars of a prison.

It was evident from the Orb's dark prison motif that Max's experience that day was unlikely to be a pleasant one, yet for Max, the physical symptoms had become so intense that his need to relieve the "hunger" for an Orb outweighed all his anxiety over what it would be like inside the Orb. So, putting well-founded apprehension aside, he braced himself for the worst, clamped his eyes shut as though that would help, held his breath, and touched his nose to the Orb.

Within moments, the Orb had settled around Max's head like a thick, dark cloak, making it impossible for Max to see anything within the Orb or outside it. But what could not be seen could be felt. The tentacles that had gathered at the base of the Orb slithered past it and down Max's neck like little lizard creatures with sharp nail-like claws pinching hard against Max's skin. The pressing made it difficult to breathe, which was already of considerable concern. But at the forefront of Max's mind was the continued migration of the tentacles as they slipped under his shirt, wrapping themselves around his upper arms and chest. The largest and slimiest of the tentacles affixed itself to Max's spine, crossing his abdomen to form a lasso at the belly. Max wriggled helplessly but could not dislodge himself from the relentless grip of the myriad appendages that at this point had spread in all directions in their march to dominate and subdue his entire body limb by limb. By the time their work was done, the bonds were so firm that no part of his body could move even an inch, and it hurt terribly to breathe.

As Max struggled against the weight of the tentacles, the thick black gave way suddenly to a flood of light so intense that it was almost as impossible to see as it had been before, especially at first, while Max's eyes were still fully dilated. Only by squinting could Max make out his surroundings enough to see the silhouette of an object approaching. The silhouette looked more like a piece of cardboard cut out in the shape of a person than it did an actual person, but it didn't take long for Max to ascertain by the size and gait of the object before him that this particular silhouette was, or represented, Emile. The silhouette approached and stood a few inches away from Max, who was still trying desperately to break away.

"Hi, Max," it said.

"Emy? Is that you?" he asked, the sound of his voice reverberating through the Orb in ever-increasing intensity.

"Of course, course...it is, is, is...Max, Max, Max," it echoed. The silhouette reached to the floor and picked up the end of the tentacle that had lassoed itself around Max's midsection. "Now, now, it is time, time, time...for your punishment, punishment, punishment, punishment..."

"Emy, Emy, Emy...no! no! no..."

The silhouette ignored Max as it rigorously tugged at the appendage. This caused the part of the tentacle that was lassoed at the belly to constrict violently, forcing out the air in Max's stomach. Reeling in pain, Max gasped for a breath of air and fought the impulse to throw up. He was determined not to reward his oppressor with that indignity.

Max could barely think. "Please stop, stop, stop..." he pleaded.

But the silhouette did not stop; in fact, it multiplied. Now, instead of just one Emile look-alike, there were twenty or thirty (exactly how many, Max couldn't count), each holding a silver appendage and tugging violently at it. The pain was unreal, and Max whimpered helplessly. There was no point in struggling. This went on for an hour, though, to Max, it seemed like days while the intensity of the experience was at its peak. Then it ended. As the bright lights grew dim, the tentacles lost their grip and melted into vapor. The silhouettes vanished, and all that was left was an exhausted body soaked in sweat.

CHAPTER 36

Saturday gave Max time both to recover from the ordeal and to ponder and reevaluate his situation. He was furious with the Box, and with himself, and even with Emy, yet he was helpless to do anything to solve his plight. *I'm so much smarter than Emy,* Max thought, *so how did he manage to break away from his glass so easily while I'm still stuck with the Box?*

As for the Box, it slept until about midday. When it woke up, it was back to its chipper and chatty self, bantering with Max as though they were best buddies. In fact, this seemed to be the Box's charm-and-harm signature, Max suddenly realized. On a dime, its delightful, happy-go-lucky demeanor would give way to the unleashing of a violent storm of nasty insults and punishments, only to be followed by affectionate and genial affability and sometimes even remorse. So when the Box turned "nice" again, Max understood the ruse and played along, not so much to grovel for more Orbs, but rather to buy time to plan his attack. After all, the Box's behavior wasn't likely to change for the better and, Max figured, it was just a matter of time before it would have its next tantrum, or worse, force Max to do something drastic like harm Emy. *Orbs or no Orbs*, Max decided, *I'm finished with this Box. I'm going to kill it.*

The Box itself was made of hard wood, and Max wasn't entirely sure he would be capable of crushing it hard enough in one blow with a hammer. True, Emile had smashed his with a hammer, but that was a piece of glass, not hard wood, which might not crack so easily. Max seriously considered just ditching the Box in the woods, but he was afraid that either it would somehow find its way back and attack him, or that he himself would go out in search of it when the cravings for a new Orb became too hard to endure.

No, it has to be destroyed completely. But how? If only I had Gryffindor's sword or some basilisk venom. *Or even some fiendfyre. Fiendfyre? Hey, I don't have fiendfyre, but I could make a really good, ordinary muggle-fire! Maybe that would work? That's what I'll do; I'll barbecue it to death! Teriyaki Terminus. Sounds delicious!*

Max and his mom didn't own a barbecue, and while his apartment building had once had outside pits for tenants to use, the landlord had banned them a few years ago after someone's kid fell into one and got hurt. But Max had seen a barbecue somewhere. *In fact*, he mused, *I tripped over one in the clearing at the tracks!* A scar on his ankle still testified to that. It was an old barbecue, and Max wasn't sure of its condition, but he could probably prop it up with a few bricks and use it as a basin for the fire. And there in the clearing, he would be just a few steps from the gate where he could make a quick escape and get back onto the main street if attacked by any of the creatures in there. At the same time, the clearing would offer much-needed privacy to hide from nosy neighbors who might ask uncomfortable questions or make complaints. There would also be plenty of old scraps of discarded wood there in the clearing to keep a fire going long enough to destroy the Box.

Max figured he would be able to resist the Box best early in the day before cravings set in. He would take the Box to the clearing Sunday morning as soon as his mom was out of the house. He would need matches and maybe some towels to clean up afterward, but not much else, so he packed everything into a bag along with some food and a bottle of water and waited up for what would hopefully be the last Orb of his life.

When the Orb finally appeared, Max eyed it stoically. *How will I cope when the Box is gone?* At first, Max was reluctant to partake of it, but as the Orb hovered gently in midair within just inches of his nose, beckoning him to submit to its allure, Max realized that as long as the Box was around, he really didn't have any choice in the matter. In the course of the Box's tenure, Max had ceded his independence of both mind and body and forfeited *his* destiny to *its* whims and desires. Max reached out and touched the Orb.

CHAPTER 37

This final Orb was magnificent, so beyond-beyond in scope that it seemed deliberate—perhaps a redress or atonement for the Box's prior tantrum—or perhaps the Box sensed Max's change in attitude and was trying to lock in his affections. When the mist lifted, revealing the Dream Hacker dashboard, Max had already planned where his final dream hacking job would take him. After all, he had rarely summoned the courage in real life to confront the Box directly, and for that matter, he still understood strikingly little of its inner workings. *What if burning it doesn't work?* Max pondered as the Box lay asleep on his desk, snoring loudly.

"Dream Hacker is now ready. Name your target."

"The Box," Max declared.

Dream Hacker paused momentarily, as if questioning the wisdom of hacking into the dreams of the chief sorcerer itself. Evidently, though, it allowed Max to proceed. The mist lifted, revealing a stunning, red-tiled infinity pool and an adjacent bar-deck dotted with black-and-silver-strapped lounge chairs, each unoccupied but for the one at the far end of the deck.

A voice roared, "Max, where are you? Get over here!" Max froze. He had certainly not deployed the "hack as self" module and should only have been present as an invisible observer.

A voice resembling his own replied, "I'm coming, I'm coming!"

"Hurry up. Now! Bring me my Coke."

Max turned toward the sound of his voice as a dream version of himself came into view, emerging from the bar and carrying a cup with a straw and a bottle. He watched as his twin strode across the terrace, clad in a pair of brown swim trunks and a small cap. The blossoming sunburn adorning the rest of his body caused the real Max to wince.

"You got me the wrong Coke!" the Box bellowed. This one is made of corn syrup. I told you I want the Coke in the GLASS bottle—the kind made with real sugar!"

"You never said it had to be glass," the boy answered as the real Max's blood boiled.

"You just weren't listening, you liar. Now, do what you're told."

As the submissive dream-Max withdrew with the unused bottle, the real Max glanced furiously at the meter. *Good. I've still got half my time.*

"Hack as self!" Max called, and at once he became his own dream-twin and returned to the lounge to take on the Box.

"Where's my Coke?" the Box spat.

"Go get it yourself," Max retorted, his voice loud and high. "I'm not your slave."

The Box vibrated ominously. "You're worse than a slave after all I've done for you."

"All you've done is ruined me! You're the most horrible thing on earth."

The Box purred quietly. "That's absurd; you're a nutcase. You know perfectly well that everything I did for you…everything…was what you asked for…even begged for. How about the hours I spent doing your homework when you didn't want to?"

Max sighed. "You made me cheat! I never cheated before."

The Box laughed. "Since when did I make you cheat, you imbecile? You're the one who sat there rubbing me against your stupid paper! Any idea how it feels to be wiped against a hard surface for two hours? You could've just *done the work* in half that time! I should never have offered my services to *you*!"

It was true, Max had to admit, that the Box had only done the things Max had asked. It had all felt so good.

"That doesn't mean you had to give it to me," Max pointed out defensively.

"So you're angry at me for being too nice. Well, *sorrry*," it added contemptuously, "I'm not going to apologize because you're too much of a loser to appreciate what I've done for you. Now go make me some french fries, and be sure they're crispy and definitely not burnt. I *hate* burnt food."

By the time Max finally returned with the food, armed with new salvos to support his side of the argument, the Box's mood had completely changed, and there was no room for further discussion.

"The fries are perfect. Good job, Max-old-boy!"

On that, the scene turned grey and the Orb vanished. Confused and disoriented by the Box's manipulation, Max realized that the Box had done it again-- it had twisted things around to make it seem as though Max himself was the bad guy, the source of all his own problems, while the Box was the good guy. It even had Max serving it refreshments and abusing him for it.

Suddenly, the Box's dream scenario seemed to snap into a new focus. Instead of seeing it from his own perspective, Max realized that the Box's dream revealed the ugly truth Max had long suspected: the Box wasn't seeing Max as a friend, an equal. It saw him as a lower being, existing only to serve as a punching bag. The Box considered Max worthless, and Max had almost started believing it. Max felt hot and defiant, and determined to move forward. *I've got to go through with it once and for all.*

CHAPTER 38

I t took his mom longer to get out the next morning than Max expected, but there were still at least six hours before he would begin to crave another Orb, which would give him ample time to kindle a decent-sized fire and perform his deed. Pocketing the Box carefully so that it would not wake up, Max grabbed his bag and headed over to the gate that opened into the clearing. He slipped inside.

Max had never been to the tracks in the morning, so this was his first time seeing it fully lit by the sun, which at this hour was unobstructed by the utility buildings. Even when drenched in light, though, the tracks still cast an uncomfortably eerie feeling, helped by the gusts of wind and the hum of the transformers and wires overhead, which were difficult to ignore. The barbecue lay in a few pieces on the ground when Max got there, but was easily reassembled and then loaded with wood and other flammable detritus that Max found strewn on the ground here and there in every assortment of size and shape. Max pressed on with the fire preparation, all the while assuming that the Box was probably still asleep in his pocket. Lighting the fire proved challenging against the adversarial winds, and even after getting a match to ignite, Max had trouble kindling a decent flame. But eventually, with the help of a makeshift wind screen, he succeeded in building a fire with enough staying power and heat to incinerate the Box.

Max hoped that the Box would sleep through this ordeal, but, in fact, when Max pulled it out from his pocket, it was wide awake, abundantly cheerful, and in an all-around really terrific mood.

"Is that the smell of fire?" it purred.

"Um, yeah. I'm, uh, making a barbecue. Teriyaki. Um. Want some when it's done?"

"You know I don't eat," the Box replied, "but I'm really happy for you if you get a nice meal, considering, that is, how much you put up with me. You deserve the best!"

Max looked down, then at the fire, and back at the Box.

The Box yawned. "I am going to prepare the most beautiful Orb for you tonight. I hope you like it."

Max added some twigs and stoked the flames. "That's so nice of you. Um, I'm sure I will."

"Would you prefer turquoise Mind Glitter today or the usual magenta mixed with green and white?"

The fire looked fully stoked and ready. "Oh, um. Either is fine."

It's just a Box, Max thought, *a lousy Box. Why do I feel like such a heel?*

"I don't smell meat. Did you put it on yet? Do hurry, please, so we can get out of here. I don't like fires; I'm made of wood, you know."

His hands shaking, Max tossed in some dry brush. *Think of the times when it's not like this*, Max thought. *I'm scared of it every second of the day, and it has complete control of me. Forget the Mind Glitter and the Dream Steam. I have to stop this thing now. If Emy could do it, I can too! Can't I?*

"You forgive me for the times I've been mean to you, right? I can't help it, you know. And I'm only doing it for your own good."

The "forgiving" thing was too much for Max to take. *This Box was more than just mean*, Max thought, *and it's trying to weasel its way out. It wants to confuse me and get me to feel bad for it! It knows perfectly well what I'm about to do.*

And on that note, without sparing a moment for reconsideration, Max plunged the Box into the fire and pulled a few steps back for safety. He watched the flames flicker against the contours of the Box and waited. And waited. And waited. There were no dramatic death scenes, pyrotechnics, or cinematic sound effects. Just silence.

CHAPTER 39

Fifteen, twenty, twenty-five minutes later. The Box, still immersed in flames, appeared totally intact and unscathed. This was not good.

With the Box still buried in flames and Max unwilling to go near it, the stalemate went on. Five minutes more, and then, without fanfare, a small Orb, almost completely transparent, alluringly iridescent like a soap bubble, rose from the flames. Max froze. It climbed to a height overhead and slipped quickly to the front of the exit gate, where it blocked a potential escape back to the street.

This was *very* not good.

Max knew he mustn't touch that Orb, so he turned to the path that led into the tracks as the only other means of escape. To his dismay, strategically positioned at that curve in the road, were two individuals of distressingly questionable intent: one big guy holding something that looked like a small shard of glass, and next to him, a short fellow with a big smirk on his face. It dawned on Max that the shard of glass in the big one's hand must be yet another of the Box's glass "offspring," and that the Box must have contacted the two ruffians by communicating through the glass and asking them to come to its aid.

"Baby says Mama gonna be awful cross bein' put in that fire," the short one said to the taller one, loud enough for Max to hear. "Mama's only made o' wood, you know."

"Yeah, Shorty. I wonder who'd do a thing like that to Mama." He glared at Max malevolently.

Terror-struck, Max's subconscious took over, and the immediate autopilot decision was made to dodge the Orb and escape through the exit rather than deal with this Shorty guy and his friend and then have to run the full length of the tracks to get out on the other side. So Max lunged toward the gate where the Orb stood guard, and in a brief, life-or-death game of tag, tried in vain to outsmart the Orb into veering to one side long enough for Max to tumble his way in a quick shift of direction through the gate without touching it. This proved to be impossible, and to Max's sheer consternation, the Orb advanced toward him threateningly.

As the Orb drew near, Max instinctively shot out his right arm and swatted at it as though it were a fly, but the Orb didn't veer off as an insect would. Instead, it grasped onto and encompassed Max's fist, forming a full-circle halo around it. Max desperately tried to fling the Orb off his hand, but despite the effort, it would not let go. On the contrary:

it affixed itself even more firmly and pulled, fist and all, tenaciously towards Max's nose. With as much strength as he could yield, Max sought to pull his arm away, but the Orb countered by short-circuiting the muscles in Max's arm, causing them to cramp up as Max pushed to keep the Orb out of range of his face. All efforts failed. As Max's arm fully gave out, the Orb thrusted victoriously to its target, and Max was once again under the Box's spell.

CHAPTER 40

Max's body went limp as though it had been injected with snake venom, and he fell to the ground with a thump to the hoots and howls of Shorty and his friend, who stood there pointing. Max looked up, taking notice of the barbecue where, to his dismay, the Box, which he had originally taken for dead, could be observed crawling along the perimeter of the grill. It had grown to many times its size, and had sprouted at least six black, hairy legs on which to walk. At the midpoint of the Box sat a giant eyeball, red with fury, which glared wildly, flitting in one direction and then the next. Just below the eyeball, a blackened tongue shot out like that of a lizard. It was then that the Box caught, or produced, a long, thin thread on which it slid, like a zip line, across from the barbecue's basin to Max's head, where it alighted and crawled onto Max's right ear. Max gave out a shallow yelp as a screeching voice penetrated deeply:

"You have betrayed me! Now you will hunger for Orbs

every minute of the day and will do my bidding or get nothing. You are powerless against me."

What happened after that was hazy, though Max recalled somehow stumbling home and into his bedroom. The Box had returned to its normal size and the hairy legs, the eyes, and the tongue were gone. Apparently, the Box Spider thing had been merely a hallucination fabricated by the Bubble Orb he had been forced to ingest in the clearing.

Over the next two days, true to the Box's word, there was no respite from the constant thirst for the next Orb. Consequently, Max fell severely behind in his schoolwork and could barely concentrate during class.

This thing is much bigger than I am, Max thought. *I can't fight the Box on my own! I feel so alone. I wish I had someone to fight it with me.* This was a hard conversation for Max to have with himself, because Max was very much not the type of kid to ever ask for help. *There's nothing wrong with me for needing help, is there? If I ask for help, everyone will know what a failure I am. But if I don't, I think I might actually die. Emy asked for help, but I'm smarter than he is. Well, I'm kind of dumber, actually.*

The Box was in Max's pocket, as usual, and rarely left him alone other than at night. So in Mr. North's class, when the teacher instructed everyone to take notes on Plato's allegory of the cave, Max seized the opportunity to take his own notes—not about Greek philosophy, but about the Box. As hard as it was to admit, Max realized his only hope was to ask his friends, teachers, and, as a last resort, maybe even his mom, for help. For now, a note to Emy would have to do.

Yo, help me out asap! Remember ur dish? I have the same but worse i'm serious. CANT GET RID OF IT! It's super mad@u for smashing the glass!!! Hears/smells thru pockets, careful when near me. Nothing feels safe anymore. Dont tell my mom! Emy help ASAP! Bring some1 hu knos what2do. 2nite my apt lobby 9pm. URGENT!!!!

CHAPTER 41

It had been a hard day for Emile. Besides the C- on the science test he had studied three hours for last night, the "incomplete" on the essay from last week because he only wrote two paragraphs instead of three, and having no clue what the lesson was about in math today, he was also sick from watching Max, his best friend, fade away into his own world. Emile really looked up to Max, and though, admittedly, sometimes he did get a little jealous, he was mostly proud of how smart Max was. Max hardly had to study for tests. He read books at practically the speed of light, remembering everything he took in. And he got straight As even though he never had to work hard. In fact, Max was just the kid Emy thought his own parents would have wanted him to be. Yet all that had changed in just the last few months. True, Max still seemed to do his homework and pass tests, but during class, he mostly just sat there like a zombie. Even the walks home with Max were awkward.

Max gazed at things with an odd expression on his face as though he were deep in a trance, sometimes turning suddenly behind him as though he thought he were being followed. Being with Max got to be so uncomfortable that Emile had already started looking for excuses to stay at school late just to avoid having to walk with him. This day was no exception, and when Emile went to his locker after PE, he was so deep in thought, trying to plan how he might *avoid* Max, that he almost didn't notice a sheet of paper that had fallen to the floor of his locker. Fortunately, the paper had come to rest on a Ziploc bag full of uneaten orange slices from lunch, and Emile, who was hungry enough at that hour even for fruit, noticed it there and gave it a read.

"Yo, help me out asap!"

Who's this from? Hey, this is Max's writing! How long has this been here?

"Remember ur dish? I have the same but worse. CANT GET RID OF IT! It's super mad@u for smashing the glass!!!"

The glass dish I smashed. Oh no!

"Hears, smells thru pockets, careful when near me. Dont tell my mom! Bring some1 hu knos what2do. 2nite my apt lobby 9pm. URGENT!!!!"

Emile read the paper over and over, just to make sure he got what it said right, and he wiped away a tear. He knew perfectly well how controlling the glass had been and how hard it had been to tear himself away from it. *Max would never joke like this! What do I do? It says not to say anything in front of it. OK, fine, I won't. He wants help. He needs some-one. Who? Who do I know? Who would I go to if I needed help? Well… easy. I'd go to my parents. But he says not to go to his mom, so that's out. I can't ask him what to do, so I have to make a decision. Who here at the school would be able to help him at 9 tonight? What about Mr. North? He's our grade counselor, so he should know what to do. I won-der if he'll believe me.*

CHAPTER 42

The relationship between Max and the Box did not recover after the failed barbecue assassination attempt the way it had in previous instances of so-called misunderstandings between them. As far as the Box was concerned, Max was eternally accountable and guilty of treachery for trying to do it in. Its Orbs reflected that animosity in the rough texture of each respective outer sphere, which was thick like elephant skin and lacked color besides some dismal grey and an awful-looking, putrid shade of yellow. The Orbs offered no Mind Glitter or Dream Steam and never gave Max that feeling of satiation he craved. Instead, the Box dished out hefty doses of silent treatment punctuated by periodic grunts and disparaging comments throughout the day. Because of its deep distrust, it insisted on being in Max's pocket at all times with no exceptions, other than at night when it needed fresh air from the open window to get decent sleep. Thus, at about 8:20 p.m., Max placed the Box on his desk, got into bed on the pretense of going to sleep, and then listened intently for signs that the Box had nodded off. Max figured it would take about twenty minutes for that to happen, so with twice that time available, he felt as confident as possible that by 9:00 p.m., the Box would be deep enough in slumber for him to slip out unnoticed. All went as planned, and at 9:00 p.m., Max surreptitiously left the confines of his bedroom and headed downstairs to the lobby, still in pajamas.

Max had been rehearsing all afternoon for what he would say to whomever showed up that evening in the lobby—and, as he walked down the stairs, he repeated again and again from memory his well-practiced speech. It covered everything that had transpired over the months having to do with the Box, and even included the parts of the story that were unpleasant to admit, like going through the tracks without permission and taking the broken bicycle, stealing his mom's mirror and then the glass from the store, and, most embarrassingly, all of the bad decision-making and the fact of his being under the control of this awful thing for so long.

So, when Max reached the lobby at 9:02 p.m., he was completely prepared, or at least he thought he was, in terms of what he was planning to say. What actually happened, however, was a different story.

The figure of a man turned toward him. At first, Max

didn't recognize him in the dark of the poorly lit lobby, but as his eyes adjusted to the dim light, he saw that it was none other than Mr. North gazing at Max with a very sincere I-really-know-how-to-understand-kids expression on his face. He then took a step closer to Max so that he and Max were within arm's distance of each other, while Max, clad in pajamas, mustered the courage to speak. But when Max tried to convey his well-rehearsed speech, to his surprise, all that moved was his mouth, while the sound of his voice just disappeared into the air. He took a deep breath and tried again, but to no avail.

Now I'm making a fool of myself in front of my teacher, Max thought despondently.

For Max, this was the end. Realizing he had failed again, his eyes welled up in tears and his face went limp, flushed and red. In despair, Max reached out to Mr. North, wrapped his arms around him in a tight hug, and sobbed for the first time he could remember. Every feeling he had contained or suppressed—the Box, the shame and embarrassment, being a thief, and, like the Box always said, being a nobody…it all came flooding to the surface in a tidal wave of remorse and self-incrimination. Max buried his face in Mr. North's suit jacket and kept sobbing.

"Help. Help me. Please. Please."

Mr. North embraced Max, waiting while he gained his composure, and as Max relaxed, said, "I would like to understand what has happened, Max. Can you tell me?"

Max shuddered. "It's the Box. I was given this Box that has these Orbs that make me feel good and see things that aren't there, and get into people's dreams. But it's mean, and calls me names, and makes me do things I don't want to do. I can't help it!"

"Max. Where is this box now?"

"It's upstairs sleeping. That's why I could come down here now. Otherwise, it's always in my pocket and listens to what I say. If it finds out I'm talking to you, I'm finished."

"Nobody is going to find out, Max. What about your friend Emy? He says he had one of these things, too?"

"Yeah, but his was a glass dish and he smashed it. Mine's wood. Mustache, um, I mean, Roxanne Buckfort. She has a mirror that's just like it. The Box created it for her from, um, a pocket mirror."

"Her mirror also has these controlling powers?"

"I'm pretty sure it does," Max said, "but hers isn't as strong as the Box, as far as I can tell. At least not yet." Max looked at his watch. "I've gotta go! It's already almost 9:30, and it's gonna wake up soon and listen to make sure I'm in my room! It can hear me breathe, and if I'm not there..." Max made a cutting gesture with his finger across his neck.

"But, Max, are you sure this box can really do all these things?"

"What—do you think I'm making this up? I'm not making things up! Forget it. I've got to get up there right now!"

"OK, Max. Here. Take my phone number. You can call

anytime. Emy has it, too. Can we meet again tomorrow, here? I want to help you, Max."

Max took the card with Mr. North's number. "I don't know. Yeah. I'll come down again tomorrow. I mean, maybe." Grateful that his teacher had come to help, but bitterly disappointed that Mr. North had done nothing real, or even believed him, Max thanked Mr. North for coming to see him and raced back upstairs.

CHAPTER 43

Whatever the Box had put into Max's Orb that night had the boy in a stupor for most of the next morning, not that anyone noticed. At school, most of the kids' attention was directed at Mustache. Roxie had lost a considerable amount of weight, so much so that her cheeks had sunken into her face, and the rest of her body had come to resemble a No. 2 pencil, the bushel of her pink-dyed hair serving as the eraser. The odd thing was that she seemed to consider her emaciated body physically attractive. Taco, who was naturally really skinny, seemed to like it, but he was the only one. But today, Mustache had fainted in the bathroom during first period, barely avoiding hitting her head against the sink in the process.

When Mustache was called out of class during history, everyone assumed it was so that Mrs. Xavier, the school nurse, could check her out again to make sure she was still OK after the earlier fall. But in actuality, it was Mr. North who had called Mustache to his office. By 3:00 p.m., Max was more alert as the effects of the previous Orb began to fade, but he also began painfully craving his next Orb, just as the Box had said would happen.

For its part, the Box sat quietly in Max's pocket. Its disposition changed, however, about fifteen minutes after Mustache had been called, when Max suddenly felt heat radiating against the skin of his right leg.

Now what? Max thought.

The reason behind the Box's sudden change of mood only became apparent when Mustache returned a few minutes later, totally distraught.

"Mr. North took away my mirror," she bawled, retreating into her chair and breathing heavily.

While the rest of the class rolled their eyes at her, it took a moment for the implications of her statement to sink in for Max. When it did, Max's face went white. He turned back and saw that Emile's face reflected his own horror.

"It knows," Max mouthed to his friend, gesturing to his pocket. "He's got the mirror."

When the dismissal bell finally rang, Emile raced to Mr. North's office to warn him not to talk to the mirror, but Mr. North had already left for the day. Berating himself for not having the paper with the teacher's phone number, Emile rushed back to catch up with Max, only to discover, to his dismay, that Max was gone.

CHAPTER 44

On a scale of one to ten, the Box's anger level would easily have registered over a thousand. It was totally livid, and its heat had become so intense that Max had no choice but to stick wads of paper towels in his pocket and hurry home to grab a pot holder to lift the Box out of his pocket before his pants caught fire.

"Use your grimy little hands, you swine," the Box said while Max extracted it and put it on his desk.

"What do you want from me?" Max pouted.

"We're leaving," the Box said. "*You* told North about me. That's a violation of my rules, and now we have to leave. We're going to Uptown. Get your stuff. Now!"

Max couldn't understand why he felt so compelled to comply with the Box's demands. But he did, nonetheless, and as much as he did not *want* to leave home, he followed the instructions as the Box told him, and within a few minutes they were out the door, rushing in the direction of the bus station.

The Box cooled off enough to be touched and insisted that Max keep hold of it at all times so that it could listen for signs of further treachery. Thus, Max carried it even as they left the building and headed up the street. Emile, who had just found Mr. North's home phone number in a pocket of yesterday's pants which he had retrieved from the hamper, glanced out of his bedroom window to the street as Max and the Box passed by. Emile shot after them just in time to see Max crossing to the central bus terminal and entering the gate for the #3 to Uptown.

Mirror or no mirror, Emile had to tell Mr. North. Hands shaking, Emile dialed the number on the paper.

"Mr. North! You've gotta help! Max ran away! He's on the #3 bus headed to Uptown!" Emile gasped. "Oh, and whatever you do, DON'T tell the mirror ANYTHING!"

Mr. North looked incredulously at Roxanne Buckfort's mirror, which was resting on the nightstand next to him. "OK, Emy. I won't say a word to the mirror."

CHAPTER 45

The first stop on the #3 was particularly busy that day, and so the bus stood idling for about five minutes loading an influx of new riders. Max, who was sitting near the back, waited in sort of a trance, staring blankly out of the window at all the strangers. Then, out of nowhere, the Box piped up.

"Get off the bus!" it snapped. "We've been spotted."

Max jumped up, and quickly disembarked. "Where are we going?"

"Just do exactly what I tell you, boy. Start walking back toward your house and keep near the bushes!"

Max turned back, away from the direction of the bus, and began walking toward his house as instructed. Two, then three police vehicles whizzed by, and Max wondered if they had been sent to save him. In a short time, Max passed the bus terminal, crossed at the light, and headed back along Reeves Street toward his apartment. Once they reached it, though, the Box barked yet another command.

"Cross the street!"

"Why?" Max said. He crossed the street and at once realized where the Box was taking him. "No, not in there!"

"You're done for, boy."

Submissively, Max entered the clearing, hopeless that anyone would ever find him.

CHAPTER 46

L et's see where your idiot friends are," the Box said curtly as it tuned in to a live audio broadcast from the mirror that Mr. North had brought with him in his pocket.

Mr. North's voice rang through. "*Zzstzh*…he must have gotten off the bus at the last stop, *zzstzh*."

"*Zzstzh*…maybe he had second thoughts and decided to go home," another man suggested. "I'll send one of my officers to check it out."

Mr. North turned to Emile. "Who else does Max hang out with?"

"Mostly just me and Swagger." Emile pulled out his phone. "I'll call, but I guarantee you Max won't be there. Max is only gonna go where the Box tells him to go."

Mr. North frowned. "OK, Emy. Where would *the Box* tell Max to go?"

"Dunno," Emile said, "though, come to think of it, maybe

they went back to the tracks where Max probably found the Box in the first place?"

Mr. North looked out in that direction. "That's brilliant, Emy. Let's go see if you're right!"

Emile still had Swagger on the phone. "Hey Swag, we're heading over to the tracks…the gate across from Max's house. OK? Meet you there!"

The Box chuckled. "So what if your friends come! All they will find is your dead body." At once, the Box produced two Orbs—one gold and one silver. "It's your choice," it purred. "Choose the Gold Orb, and you stay alive, but it will cost you. Reject my offer, and I'll force you to take the Silver Orb, and you die."

Max wasn't about to do any more "business" with the Box, but he thought it wise to keep the conversation going in the hope of buying time for his friends to get there. At least that way he wouldn't die alone.

"So what do I have to 'pay you' for the Gold Orb?" he asked.

The Box sniggered. "You take the Gold Orb, and I spare your life. And you pay with your Dreams and Aspirations."

At once Max realized the full implication of what the Box had told him months earlier:

"I am no Horcrux," it had said. "I embody the dreams and aspirations of many souls."

Apparently, Max wasn't the first one to be victimized by the Box and its evil Orbs, and Max shuddered to think what life would be like without his hopes and dreams. *Better to die than to live without hope.*

Max glared at the Box, which he still clutched in his left hand. "I know I've made bad decisions, but that doesn't mean I have to keep making them now. I'm not taking your stupid offer. I'd rather die."

"Have it your way," the Box spat.

Max swatted at the Silver Orb as it approached, and once again, instead of deflecting into the air, the Orb settled on and affixed itself to Max's right fist. It went immediately to work eroding the muscles and their power to resist its pull. In an effort to lend defensive support, Max swung his left hand over to his right arm and pushed outward with all his might, but with the Box hanging on to his left hand, he couldn't use that hand to get a solid grip on his arm, so the effort failed. Max tried whipping his hand at the ground to get the Box to fall, but it wouldn't let go. So there he stood, an Orb clinging in his right hand and the Box clutched in his left. As a last-ditch attempt to free at least one hand, Max tried smacking the Box against the Orb by striking his two hands against each other. This was the first move that seemed to get the Orb's attention, and for a moment it stopped pushing, at least long enough for Max to catch his breath. To continue this line of attack, Max clasped and then clenched his two hands in a tight grip without letting go. This resulted in the Orb having to choose between which of Max's fists to settle on. It shifted

violently back and forth between the two hands while trying to encase both hands at the same time.

Max gradually realized that he could no longer feel the
physical presence of the Box in his hand, though he could
still make out its outline within the Orb as it fleeted back
and forth between hands. The Orb continued eroding Max's
muscle strength to the extent that, finally, he had no choice
but to release his grip. When all was said and done, the Box
and the Orb had fused into one rather dangerous opponent,
still clinging tenaciously to Max's fist and still forcing its
way toward to his face.

CHAPTER 47

It was at that moment that Swagger came speeding into the clearing on his bike, followed by Mr. North and Emile, who had raced there on foot.

"Get it away from me!" Max cried. "If it touches my face, I'm dead."

Emile and Mr. North stood there, dumbfounded, staring at the bizarre, illuminated sphere encasing Max's fist. But Swagger was unphased. To Swagger, a round object *always* meant "something to throw," by definition.

"Pass it here, Max!" Swagger cried.

Um, OK. Worth a try, Max thought.

Grasping his weak right arm with his left hand as though holding a bat, Max employed the use of his left arm muscles, their strength so far less affected by the Orb, to power a forceful swing of the right arm. And for a brief moment, the Orb actually lost its grip and was suspended in the air. It quickly rebounded, though, and reaffixed itself to Max's

fist. He tried again as Swagger drew a few feet closer. This time, the Orb made it into the air about midway between Max and Swagger before rebounding to Max. Taking another few steps forward, Swagger extended his arm out, pointing his fist directly at Max in an attempt to attract the Orb like a lightning rod.

"Try again, Max! Hard as you can!"

Applying every ounce of strength that he could muster, Max pitched hard, and the Orb flew out in a beeline, catching Swagger right in the fist. Unhappy at this turn of events, the Orb turned angry red and began to burn hot.

"It's heating up, Max," Swagger said, shaking his arm violently. "I've gotta get this moron off me, pronto."

Emile moved into position. "Pass it here, Swag!"

Soon they were passing it back and forth between them as Max stood on the sidelines. Even the incredulous Mr. North took a few turns catching the Orb.

The next few minutes were a wild spectacle that one would have to witness to believe it could possibly be true—two boys and a fully grown adult playing a dangerous game of catch with an illuminated sphere.

The Orb's temperature kept rising to the point that it burned even to the briefest touch, and on Emile's turn with the Orb, he recoiled. "It's too hot! What do I do, Swag?"

"Pass it here," Swagger said, not knowing exactly what he was going to do with the thing either.

Emile pitched the Orb to Swagger. At this point, the Orb

was scorching, and Swagger, not a friend to anything re-sembling pain, shrieked in agony. He thought to escape the clearing—at least that would get the Orb away from Max—but that plan was quickly deterred by the sudden appear-ance of a short, unsavory individual wearing a smirk who showed up from nowhere and barred the way. The other route from the clearing was blocked by a larger, unwanted guest holding a shard of glass. So Swagger just ran in cir-cles, screaming his head off in pain.

The interesting thing about Swagger was that, although his academic performance in school was truly abysmal, to say the least, not to mention his lack of attentiveness and focus—which was just plain, well, sad—when it came to being aware and in command of his environment even in the most extreme situations, nobody could hold a can-dle to him. So perhaps it was not surprising that of them all, it would be Swagger who would keep his head and no-tice, even as he was racing furiously around, that the Orb seemed to crackle slightly whenever he came within close proximity to the giant legs of the large electric transformer that stood nearby.

Swagger made another circle around the transformer tower to confirm his observation.

Hmmm, you like electricity, eh, ya overgrown nightlight? Seething in pain, Swagger positioned himself directly across from the lowest electric coil he could find on the tower and computed his aim. Then, with full confidence in his throwing abilities, he wound up for the pitch and hurled the Orb so brilliantly that the sheer force of his throw compelled the Orb to abandon its residency on Swagger's fist in favor of the electric coil some ten feet above. It flew through the air and, upon making contact, was seemingly swallowed by the electric coil above with surprisingly little fanfare. This eventuality did not look promising for Shorty and his friend, who took their cue and quickly disappeared.

This was not the end of the Orb, however. Moments later, an Orb popped up on one of the connected wires, and then another, and another, and another. Although these new Orbs did not illuminate as the original had, they clearly had the power to replicate, and they reproduced in droves, migrating along the wires like squirrels and settling at various positions along the way.

With the immediate threat abated, all eyes turned to Max, who, dazed and confused, promptly fainted, collapsing into Mr. North's arms.

CHAPTER 48

When Max woke up, he found himself lying in a hospital bed with Mr. North at his side.

"How are you feeling, Max?"

"Ugggh. My head hurts so bad. And my hands are on fire. Oh, my stomach. Cramps. It's horrible. I need an Orb!! Get me an Orb! Please…"

"There are no more Orbs, Max. Even if there were, you can't stay addicted to them anymore. You need to break the habit. You know that, right?"

"Yeah. No, it's too hard. I feel like my head is gonna explode."

"Max, I don't know what was in those Orbs, but the doctor is treating this case like any other addiction. It might take a full week, maybe even two weeks, for your body to adjust back to normal. We'll all be here to help you. Do you understand, Max?"

"Yeah, OK. Just don't tell my mom."

"Max, we've already told your mom. The hospital called her as soon as we got you here."

Max swallowed hard. "She must be so disappointed in me."

"Max, she is deeply grateful that you're alive. She is in the waiting room and wants to see you. Can she come in now?"

Max nodded, and Mr. North left the room so that Max could be alone with his mom.

"I'm sorry, Mommy. I'm so sorry!" Max slid his head into her lap and she caressed his forehead.

"It's OK, Max. You'll be OK."

"It's all my fault. I never should have taken that horrible Box in the first place."

"No, Max. It's not your fault. It's my fault for not being there for you. I'm so sorry you thought you had to deal with that awful Box on your own, sweetie. That's going to change, Max, I promise."

Instead of answering, Max motioned urgently for the trash bin and threw up globs of muck. "Owwww, my stomach!"

"Oh, dear. It's going to be OK, Max. Hang in there, OK?"

"Mommy, do you have to go right back to work? Please, can you stay with me? It hurts so much, I can't bear it alone anymore."

"I'm not going anywhere," she said firmly, handing Max a towel to wipe his mouth. "Now, get some rest."

CHAPTER 49

The entire next week was torture. Food and drink still wouldn't stay down, and Max wasn't sure whether he was more nauseated by the lack of daily Orbs, or by his disgust at himself in finding that he actually missed the Box. Of course, he didn't miss the insults and the sudden mood swings, or the pressure to betray his better judgement. But Max had gotten used to the Box's constant companionship, sarcastic humor, and listening ear, and found his days a little flat without the promise of Dream Hacking to look forward to at the end of each day. Having his mother at his side, plus Mr. North's daily visits, helped support him through the adjustment to Box-less life.

By the following week, Max felt better than he had in months. He felt more intellectually alert than he had in a long time and seemed to have regained his natural sense of serenity, which he happily accepted, feeling no loss whatsoever for the euphoria he had experienced under the influence of the Orbs.

Mr. North peeked into the room. "Max, are you up for a visit? There are some friends here who would like to see you."

Max nodded, and Mr. North came in, accompanied by Emile and Swagger. Max teared up and quickly covered his face with his blanket while he regained his composure.

"I'm so sorry for what happened, guys. You were amazing. Swag, I saw that pitch! Unbelievable! And Emy, how did you figure out where the Box was taking me? I didn't even realize it until we got there."

Emile blushed. "That's what friends are for!"

"No, really, guys," Max said, "if it hadn't been for each of you, I'd be dead. Like, not just a little dead, but really <u>dead</u>. I know I should never have taken that Box in the first place, but once it had me in its grips, I needed to ask you guys for help, and I didn't, at least not until it was almost too late."

"Swagger at your service, Max! By the way, do you think the Box is still out there somewhere?"

Max thought. "Hey, Mr. North, have you still got Roxie Buckfort's mirror? Can I see it for a minute?"

Mr. North paused on that one for a moment and then checked his pockets. "Here, Max. It's not my mirror, so just for a minute."

The scene must have been rather interesting to behold when Max's mom walked into the room and saw Max, Emile,

Swagger, and Mr. North all huddled over her grandmother's mirror, Max shouting at it.

"Hey, Box-Face! You in there? Or did you overdose on your own Orb?"

Swagger grabbed hold of the mirror. "Or maybe the SHOCK THERAPY did ya some good, eh, Box?"

The mirror remained silent, until—

"*Zzstch…Zzstch…*"

"Hey, it's talking!"

"*Zzstch*…Ahhh, you wonderful cretins. We are doing marvelously well! *Zzstch*," the Box announced. It went on. "We are finding so many new clients through the marvels of electronics. No need for the hard work of conjuring up Mind Glitter, Dream Steam, and other distractions when we have at our disposal an endless library of diverting content in the form of Netflix, YouTube, mindless video games, and useless news sites to keep our clients busy for a lifetime! You can have your dumb mirror back. I haven't got time for you anymore. Goodbye and good riddance! *Zzstch*."

Mr. North figured he had better hold on to that mirror a little longer, and after pondering the implications of what the Box had to say, decided that in the interests of children (and adults) everywhere, he had better bring this matter to the attention of law enforcement. He did so the next day, and to his surprise, received an urgent call in reply. Apparently, this was not the first they had heard of the Box, nor of its Orbs. News that the Box had infiltrated the nation's electric grid was a new, added concern, and funds were immediately released to begin tracking the Orbs.

URGENT UPDATE FOR READERS EVERYWHERE:

As of this date, Orbs have been spotted residing on electric lines throughout the world. They are often found in clusters of three or four, and typically sport a pink, orange, or white plastic-like appearance. For the safety of the children, national security experts ask that anyone, child or adult, whether on a walk or on a road trip, who happens to spy the location of a suspected Orb, should submit a sightings report urgently at the official website www.orbslayers.com. Officials are taking the matter of children's safety very seriously and are intent on tracking the whereabouts of every one of these malevolent spheres.

CHAPTER 50

Max went home the next day, and sure enough, life going forward was very different. For one thing, his mom arranged a new, later lunch hour so that Max could stop at the restaurant after school any day he wanted to. Emy was invited to come also, and they usually got a bite of dessert while they were there. She was also more open with Max regarding the circumstances of his father's departure, and together, they even attempted internet searches to try tracking down his whereabouts.

Having now experienced the Orb's abusive control, Max became keen at identifying kids who might be experiencing similar challenges, encouraging them to stand strong and, most importantly, to seek help. As for videos, sure, Max watched them for pleasure, but he never dropped his guard, always suspicious that the Box might be lurking somewhere within the screen or its circuitry with evil intent to unground him from the realities and true pleasures of life.

At school, classroom life returned to normal. Mr. North was thrilled to have the old Max back, but was much more sensitive about how much work he doled out. Interestingly, he seemed to have completely expunged the word "disappointed" from his vocabulary and never used it again with his students. Swagger especially appreciated Mr. North's change in that regard. Swagger also found out what happened regarding Adrienne and the ice cream date when Max admitted to hacking his dream.

"You did what??!"

Roxie—she would never be "Mustache" to Max again—seemed a thousand times better. Max checked in with Mr. North about her, and although Mr. North would not provide details regarding another student, he assured Max that Roxie was safe and that he was meeting with her weekly to ensure that the family was on track.

The walk home from school was arduous—Hill Street was just as steep as it had been before, but it bothered Max less. Well, maybe just a little less.

"Emy, would you be willing to go into the tracks with me one more time?" Max asked on one such walk home.

Emy stopped short. "Umm, say what? The TRACKS?!"

Emile rarely raised his voice.

"No, really. I've got something I need to do. We don't have to go in there much past the gate. Really! Tomorrow morning before class. Will you please? OK?"

"Yeah, OK. I guess."

The next day, Max and Emile entered the tracks together for the first time in months, Max rolling a bicycle by his side. He had pumped up its tires, straightened out the frame, fixed the seat, and tightened the stand.

"Hello, in there," Max called out. Something rustled in the bushes. "I fixed your bike and have it here for you. When I took it, I didn't realize it belonged to someone else. I'm returning it, and I'm truly sorry."

WARNING
ORB
ACTIVITY
AREA
FOR YOUR SAFETY AND
THE SAFETY OF OTHERS
REPORT ALL SIGHTINGS AT
www.OrbSlayers.com

GREAT NEWS FOR
TEACHERS & EDUCATORS

The Box was written to meet Common Core education standards in English language arts, grammar, vocabulary and literature.

For more information, visit

www.TheBoxBook.co

1060L

www.ingramcontent.com/pod-product-compliance
Lightning Source LLC
Chambersburg PA
CBHW070539100726
47907CB00004B/1180